A Puzzle

The snow was coming down harder now. Thick clumps of sparkling white flakes clung to the bare branches and the tangled vines in the garden. The whole yard was quickly turning white, and Elise was painfully aware of Adam standing close by, close enough to touch.

He moved a step toward her, and Elise caught her breath. She didn't understand. Adam should have been inside the house with Kelly, and instead he was here, covered with snow, smiling at her, moving closer.

"I've got to leave now," she said in a big rush, putting on her mittens. "I don't like to drive in the snow. I —"

Before she could finish her sentence, Adam moved one step nearer and took her chin in one of his hands.

"Elise, you're a puzzle to me," he said. "I wish I could understand — " He stopped short and leaned over to kiss her.

COUPLES

Books from Scholastic in the **Couples** series:

LOVESTRUCK

by M.E. Cooper

SCHOLASTIC INC.
New York Toronto London Auckland Sydney

ISBN 0-590-41262-0

12 11 10 9 8 7 6 5 4 3 2 1   7 8 9/8 0 1 2/9

Printed in the U.S.A.   01

First Scholastic printing, December 1987

Chapter 1

Happiness is independence. The bright red letters on the white pin seemed to shout to Elise Hammond from the window of a novelty shop as she and her best friend, Emily Stevens, rushed through the crowded Rose Hill Mall on an early December afternoon.

"Oh, Em, I've just got to have that pin." Elise grabbed Emily by the elbow and dragged her inside the store. "It's perfect for me. Don't you think?" Without giving Emily a chance to answer, Elise made her purchase and pinned it immediately to the collar of her new wool jacket.

"How's that for making a statement?" she asked proudly.

"Hmmm. Yes, I'd say that does the trick." Emily stepped back and assessed her friend's appearance. "I guess you want *everyone* to know how happy you are to be on your own, huh?" she asked.

"Of course." Elise's green eyes sparkled.

The two girls continued their walk down the mall corridor.

"I'm finding out, Em, that it's not so terrible to be without a boyfriend, after all." Elise swung her shoulder bag and skipped a little with each step.

Emily stopped and stared at Elise. "You could have fooled me. I thought you were kind of bummed-out for a while. I mean, after you broke up with Ben, and then when things didn't work out with Justin. . . ."

Elise smiled. "I know, I know. I was sad for a while. But being sad is definitely not my style. I think things worked out for the best in both of those relationships, and I've decided that life is great with or without a boyfriend, and I'm going to enjoy it."

"Great idea," Emily teased. "Congratulations."

"Thanks." Elise touched the pin on her collar proudly. "You are looking at the new Elise. Once a hopeless romantic, now a hardheaded, practical, career-oriented individual."

"Ms. Independent, hmmm?" Emily said, obviously trying to hide a smile. Elise had the feeling that Emily didn't believe in her newfound independence.

"I'm serious, Em. I've never been happier," Elise went on. "I have my volunteer work at the Children's Hospital, lots of terrific friends, one last exciting semester of high school, and then college to look forward to. . . ."

Emily nodded.

"Come on, Em. Just because you're so happily in love with Scott doesn't mean a single girl can't be happy. I know you guys have a great relationship. You have so much in common. And Scott's a great guy."

"I agree with you there," Emily said. "But somehow I have this feeling that before too long you'll find a terrific guy who shares your interests, too. But anyway, no one ever said that was the most important part of a relationship."

"I know." Elise laughed at a roly-poly Santa Claus with incredibly bushy eyebrows who was greeting little children in the center of the mall. "But it doesn't hurt, either."

Emily gave a surprised laugh. "Well, it might be a little difficult to meet someone who goes around saving stray animals *and* organizes charity functions *and* plans to be a social worker *and* loves to work with children *and*. . ."

"Doesn't sound impossible to me, Em," Elise joked. "There could be a guy like that, somewhere. Maybe in college."

"Well, I wouldn't hold my breath if I were you," Emily said. "On the other hand, if such a person does exist, you'll meet him!" She squeezed Elise's arm affectionately. "Come on, we have some serious shopping to do."

"You're right," Elise agreed. She immediately turned her attention to a display of pastel sweaters in a store window. "My sister would love one of those," she remarked.

"Hey, maybe we should split up for half an hour," Emily said. "I saw something I'd like to buy for this crazy friend of mine, and I don't want you tagging along."

"Okay, okay, I get the picture," Elise said. "I

have some shopping I'd like to do on my own, too."

The two girls agreed to meet in thirty minutes at the ice-cream shop and went their separate ways.

Elise sailed through the holiday crowds, humming Christmas carols and enjoying the flurry of activity around her. She took a deep breath and headed toward the pet store. She always made a point of stopping to look at the puppies before she did her shopping.

As she approached, she noticed a small crowd had gathered in front of the pet shop. To the right of the doorway, a folding table had been set up. A large sign propped up against it said, HELP US CLOSE DOWN THIS PET STORE! Elise quickened her pace to find out what was happening.

"Hey, look out," she said, as someone backed into her.

"Oh, sorry. I didn't see you. Would you mind holding this for a second?" Elise looked up into the deep, dark eyes of a very handsome boy. Startled, she took the sign he thrust into her hands as he grabbed a bunch of flyers from the table and passed them around to the group surrounding him. Then he held out a clipboard that must have contained a petition and asked everyone to sign it.

Elise turned around the poster he had handed her and saw that it read, WE WANT TO SAVE THESE ANIMALS' LIVES.

What a coincidence! Elise could hardly believe it. All her life she'd been rescuing stray animals around Everett Street, and she and Emily were just joking about how unusual it would be to find someone who cared about the things she did. It seemed that there *was* such a person, and not only that, here she was, practically face to face with him.

"Thanks for your signature," he said to each person who signed his petition. "Thanks so much. Your help is appreciated."

Elise walked around the small crowd to get a better look at this boy. He was incredibly cute. But besides that, his sincere, concerned expression made Elise certain he really *cared* about what he was doing. He was starting to seem more and more remarkable.

He had a square face, smooth, fair skin, and intelligent dark brown eyes with a glint of gold in them. His dark brown hair was thick and wavy and one stray curl fell over his forehead. He pushed it back with a strong, muscled arm and turned to face Elise. She immediately felt the color rise in her cheeks. He'd caught her staring at him!

She looked at her feet and reminded herself she wasn't interested in meeting any new boys. Not now, not when she'd just discovered how great independence really could be.

"Hey, thanks a million for holding my sign," he said, coming to stand beside Elise. He didn't take it back, however. "I thought you looked like you'd want to help out with the Animal Rights League. We need all the help we can get."

"Animal Rights League? Is that what this is?" she asked, wide-eyed. "What's going on? Why do you want to close the pet store?"

"Glad you asked." He arched an eyebrow expressively and his eyes searched Elise's face. "I'll tell you why. We have a serious problem here. This pet store is contaminated. Several puppies have died here from a virus, and we believe more will die if the owners don't close down immediately."

"That's awful," Elise said sincerely. "How long has this been going on? Will it hurt the other animals, too?"

"Adam, tell them about the cages," prompted a lady who was sitting behind the folding table. By this time another small crowd had gathered around to hear what Adam had to say.

"Right, Mrs. Phelps," he said amiably.

Adam. Elise swallowed hard and tried to pay attention, tried not to concentrate on the smooth, rich tones of Adam's voice.

"The Animal Rights League is trying to generate publicity about this problem, and that's why we're here today," he announced. "The virus that killed those puppies can't be cleaned out safely. There's no way to wipe it out except to leave the cages empty for three full months, and that means closing the store."

"You're right, young man," someone called out. "I used to work for a vet, and I know about those restrictions. Once the virus hits, the puppies don't stand a chance. They really should be removed right away."

"Well, sign our petition," Mrs. Phelps said. "If we collect enough signatures we'll be able to speed up the process."

Still holding Adam's sign, Elise went over to the table and signed the petition. She also gave her name and phone number to Mrs. Phelps so she could help the group at some future date, if necessary. This was definitely a cause she'd like to join.

She turned back to look at Adam. She was beginning to think she had seen him before, possibly in the halls of Kennedy High. He wasn't a part of Elise's crowd, but she thought she remembered seeing Scott Phillips talk to him once or twice. The crowd began to disperse and Adam approached Elise, interrupting her reverie.

"Did you sign up with us?" he asked. "You look pretty good with that sign in your hands, you know."

"Thanks." She felt herself flush again. "That's probably because I believe in what you're doing here."

Adam's brown eyes sparkled and he shuffled from one foot to the other. "Great," he said. "Then maybe you'll want to help out the cause, and we can get better acquainted."

Elise's heart started beating rapidly, and her hands suddenly felt clammy and damp. She was sure that her face was growing increasingly pink.

If Adam noticed her reaction, he was too polite to mention it. "Listen, are you free right now? I was just thinking of taking a break for a soda somewhere. . . ."

Elise was contemplating what to answer when someone shouted, "Here comes a reporter from the *Rose Hill Bulletin*." Elise turned and saw Rob Kendall, a well-known local reporter, striding briskly down the wide avenue of the mall, followed by a young photographer.

"Better take your sign back," Elise said quickly,

handing the sign to Adam. "Looks like you might get your picture in the paper."

Their hands touched for an instant, and Elise trembled. Adam's fingers rested lightly on hers a bit longer than necessary, and again, his eyes searched her face, making her feel as if he could see deep inside her, read her every thought. A shot of warmth surged through her body, and she pulled her hand away abruptly.

What was going on? She recognized this familiar feeling as the start of a major crush. How could this happen to her? She wanted to be on her own. She liked the idea of relying only on herself for a while, and she *was* determined not to come unglued over a pair of soft brown eyes and a lingering touch.

"I hope you're not going to leave," Adam said. His eyes were wide and hopeful. Did he feel the same electric vibrations she was feeling? Elise wondered.

"You'll join our protest, won't you?" he asked.

"Well, I *do* want to help, but . . ." she began, ". . . I promised to meet a friend in just a few minutes. I really have to go." As she talked, she backed away slightly, trying to put some distance between her and this boy who made her heart beat so erratically. She moved backward without thinking, her eyes never leaving his face.

CRASH! Elise realized too late she was practically on top of a cardboard display that held rubber dog bones and rawhide chews. It toppled over as soon as she backed into it. The items went flying in every direction, and Elise fell flat on her backside on top of the now-useless display case.

8

It flattened under her with a *thunk*, and Elise thought she'd never be able to look Adam in the eye again.

"Don't worry," Adam said quickly. "We'll have them picked up in no time."

Humiliated, head down, Elise stood halfway up, then bent forward to pick up a handful of bones. To her total dismay, she smashed head-on into another display, this one of pet collars. Dozens of red leather collars sailed into the air, then landed among the dog bones and chews.

People in the crowd started to giggle and snicker, and Elise wished the floor would open and swallow her up.

"There's a great shot," Rob Kendall said to his photographer. "Protesters Attempt to Destroy Pet Store — literally."

"Forget it," Adam said, stepping in front of Elise. "Don't you think she's embarrassed enough already?"

Elise was grateful to Adam, but she still felt totally ashamed of her clumsiness. If only he knew it was all his fault. He made her feel completely unsteady and off-balance, and it was a terrible feeling, she realized. And now she felt stupid and uncoordinated and as though she had interrupted the Animal Rights League's peaceful protest.

"I ought to pick these up," she mumbled, getting to her feet.

"Here, I'll help you." Adam bent down and began collecting collars. In a few minutes they had everything back in place.

Elise started to go, but Adam stopped her and said, "Well, looks like I can't take my break yet after all. I'd better stick around and make sure Kendall gets his facts straight. Maybe some other time?"

Elise tried to muster up a smile. "Sure, sure, some other time." She turned and hurried away toward the ice-cream shop without looking back.

"Hey! Wait! What's your name?" she heard Adam call after her. Well, there was no way she was going to tell him now, not after that humiliating experience. Any hopes she had had of getting to know him better were quickly dashed. She'd never be able to face him again!

"Elise, what's wrong?" Emily, waiting on line for an ice-cream cone, frowned when she saw Elise come flying toward her.

"Oh, Em, you won't believe what just happened. I made such a fool of myself," Elise said through gritted teeth. "I just had a horrible klutz attack and knocked over two display cases in the pet shop. Not one, but *two*, can you believe it?"

"Calm down, Elise. What happened?" Emily asked. "It doesn't sound like the end of the world. Something upset you?"

Elise shot her friend a dark look. Why did Emily have to be so ridiculously perceptive? Elise couldn't hide anything from her. No wonder her friend was the unofficial Dear Abby of Kennedy High, as well as advice columnist for the school paper.

"No, I wasn't upset, just clumsy," Elise lied. She couldn't tell her friend about this silly instant crush she'd just developed. It didn't make any sense, especially not after the pin she had just

10

bought and her speech earlier about the new, independent Elise.

"Well, cheer up," Emily said tactfully. "I'll treat you to a giant cone. How about Death By Chocolate? I guarantee it will make you forget about your klutz attack."

Elise grinned weakly. She knew in her heart it would take a lot more than a superchocolate cone to make her forget that boy named Adam.

Chapter 2

Fiona Stone finished doing fifteen extra pliés at the barre and decided to call it a day. She'd been working out in the huge mirrored studio of the Academy of Ballet Arts, where she'd been a student for more than a year.

Late afternoon sunlight poured in through the large western windows, casting a golden glow on the thick wooden planks of the studio floor. Through the window, Fiona could see the rooftops of Georgetown between the bare branches of the winter trees. December in Rose Hill would be lovely, she thought. Her thoughts drifted back to the year before when she'd spent her first Christmas in America. She had been miserable when she first arrived. She thought she'd never get used to Rose Hill.

Back in England, she'd been a boarding student at the Kingsmont Ballet Academy, an old, prestigious school that overlooked the sea. Fiona and her best friend, Lizzy, had dreamed of nothing but becoming members of the *corps de ballet* in the National Ballet Company.

But things hadn't gone as planned. Lizzy had been accepted and, for some reason, Fiona had not. She'd had a great audition, but someone must have been much, much better.

At first she'd been devastated over her failure. Then she'd been bitter because she'd had to join the rest of her family in the States when her father, a diplomat, was assigned to Washington, D.C. But all that seemed like a very long time ago now. She had grown to love living in America.

Her life was good here. She had no complaints, although she sometimes wondered what her life would have been like if she'd been accepted into the National in London. Here in Rose Hill she was part of a terrific crowd. She had wonderful friends at Kennedy High, and best of all, she had Jonathan Preston.

Fiona ran her fingers through her hair and slipped into her coat. Jonathan made everything worthwhile, she thought dreamily. She loved him so much that sometimes, when she was with him, she found it hard to catch her breath in a normal way. She could hardly believe how lucky she was.

"Excuse me, ma'am, can I interest you in a ride home?" She heard the familiar voice as she walked out the door of the studio. It was Jonathan. She had been so lost in her thoughts about him that she wondered for a moment if she had only imagined it. But no, there he was, waiting outside on the sidewalk.

"I'd love a ride home," Fiona said, pulling the

strap of her dance bag higher on her shoulder. "I just hope I don't have to ride in a pink car or anything." Jonathan drove a battered old Chevy convertible that he had nicknamed Big Pink.

Jonathan gave her one of his perfect smiles. "Sorry, that's all I've got today." He pretended to head for his car as if he would really drive off without her. Jonathan was tall and very good-looking, although right now his face was partially obscured, as it often was, by his Indiana Jones-style hat. Fiona thought he was perfect, and she often wondered why every girl in school wasn't fighting to take him away from her.

"Oh, no, you don't." She ran after him and spun him around to face her, then stood up on tiptoes to kiss him. Her arms instinctively reached up and encircled his neck as he placed both of his hands on her shoulders and pulled her close. Their lips came together in a long gentle kiss, and Fiona couldn't imagine anything feeling more perfect. Surely this was the absolute happiest that any person could ever be.

"Well? Can I convince you to take a ride in a pink car?" Jonathan asked when they broke apart.

"Since that's my only choice I suppose so," Fiona teased, slipping into Big Pink beside Jonathan.

They rode in silence toward Rose Hill. She stared out the window at the beginning of a glorious sunset that had turned much of the sky a vivid rose color. The air was cool, but not frigid, and it felt more like an early spring day than almost the first day of winter. Fiona was looking forward to winter in Rose Hill and could hardly wait for the first big snowstorm of the season.

"Want to come in for a bit, Jonathan?" she asked when they pulled up in front of the Stones' big white house.

"Uh-uh, I can't. I have a ton of calc homework to do." Jonathan ran his forefinger up and down Fiona's ear, then leaned over and kissed her earlobe softly. She shivered and turned to meet his lips with hers.

"Thanks for the ride. I'll talk to you later, okay? I love you."

"I love you, too," Jonathan whispered, reluctantly letting her go.

"See you later, alligator." Fiona gave him a final kiss on the tip of his nose and eased herself out of the car. She wandered up her front walk slowly, breathing in the fresh December air. It felt great to be in love.

Jonathan drove off.

Fiona paused at the mailbox, reached in, and pulled out a letter. It was addressed to her. That's odd, she thought. She didn't get that much mail, and she had received a letter from Lizzy only yesterday. Then she noticed that the cream-colored envelope was imprinted with the official address of the National Ballet Company of London.

Fiona felt her heart stop for a second. And then it began to pound loudly. She could barely catch her breath. She dropped all her things and tore open the flap with trembling fingers.

"Dear Miss Stone," the letter began, impeccably typed on stationery of the same creamy

15

bond as the envelope. The words began to blur in front of Fiona's eyes.

She blinked and started over.

"We are pleased to tell you that a position has unexpectedly become available in the corps of the National Ballet Company. . . ."

Fiona drew in a sharp breath as the sentences jumbled together on the page.

"On the strength of your audition with us last year, and on the condition that you have kept up with your dancing at a reputable ballet school, we would be delighted to offer you. . . ."

Her hand stopped trembling, and the words came into focus with amazing clarity.

"We would be delighted to offer you a place in the National Ballet, effective 1 January, if you are still interested."

Still interested!!

"I don't believe it," Fiona whispered. "But . . . I must believe it. I made it — at last!" She rolled her eyes toward the sky and let out a whoop. "I made it into the National Ballet!" She quickly clamped a hand over her mouth to keep from shouting with joy. It wasn't like her to be so vocal.

But this was incredible. She had waited half her life for this moment. Since she was five, it had been her wildest dream. But the timing was so

16

awkward now, she thought, her mind turning to Jonathan. She shivered again, remembering his gentle touch in the car.

How could she possibly leave Rose Hill? How could she move to London and leave Jonathan behind? It was impossible, and yet —

It would be impossible not to go, too. She was a dancer, first and foremost. She had always claimed ballet was the most important thing in her life. How could she turn down a chance with the National?

"Jonathan," she murmured, staring at the letter she held in her hands. "How am I ever going to make you understand?"

"Hi there, Fi," Jeremy called out to his sister as Fiona entered the house. He was sprawled out in front of the living room fireplace reading a history assignment.

"I don't know about this American history," he chattered. "Those colonists! They seem to think they had good reason to revolt against Mother England. The whole thing baffles me, Fiona, doesn't it you?"

She nodded, not trusting herself to open her mouth. She put down her books, purse, and gym bag and remained silent. She wasn't ready to tell anyone —not even her brother — the big news.

"Hey, Fi?" Jeremy questioned. "Anything wrong?" He stood up to greet her, but she turned and rushed back out the front door. "Where are you going?" he called after her.

She dashed across the front lawn as fast as she could go and headed up the street. But she was soon overtaken by her brother, who was taller and faster and much more determined than she.

"What's going on, Fi?" he demanded. "And don't tell me nothing. You look awful." Jeremy's face was serious. "Do you want to talk about it, or must I resort to an ancient form of torture?"

Fiona laughed weakly in spite of herself. Jeremy was such a nut . . . and such a kind, caring brother. She'd have to tell him sooner or later, so why not now? She took a deep breath.

"Jeremy, the most unbelievable thing has happened," she said. "I mean, the most amazing thing you could ever imagine. . . ."

"Does it have anything to do with the National Ballet?" he asked casually.

Her mouth fell open. "How did you know?"

"Because I peeked into the mailbox, of course. As soon as I saw that official-looking envelope, I stuck it back in for you to find."

"Oh, Jeremy." She stopped walking and gestured with her hands. "I'm so excited I can hardly breathe. They want me; I've finally been accepted there, after all this time!"

Jeremy gave her a giant hug. "It's stupendous. I'm so proud of you. Congratulations and — and all that stuff. How happy you must be!"

"Oh, Jeremy, I *am* happy," she said carefully. "I'm thrilled and speechless . . . and — " She broke off and her eyes filled with tears. "But I can't stop thinking of Jonathan. How can I ever, ever tell him that I'll be leaving Rose Hill for good?"

Jeremy's eyebrows went up. "Yes. I see what

18

you mean. That is a problem, isn't it?" he said. "It's going to be hard for him."

"It's even hard for me to accept, Jeremy. I've built such a wonderful life here in Rose Hill. Everything here is so perfect. . . ."

Jeremy squinted at her. "You wouldn't think of not going, would you?"

She hesitated for a moment. "No, not really," she finally said. "Dancing has always been my life, you know that. It's just that here in Rose Hill I finally had the chance to experience living the way most kids my age do, and I've loved it. But I still love ballet. I don't think this is an offer I can pass up. How am I ever going to explain it to Jonathan?"

"Well, for starters, you must be honest with him, and you must tell him right away. None of this being afraid to confront him, as you were about the prom that time." Jeremy was referring to the time when Fiona chose to dance in *Coppelia* rather than attend the prom with Jonathan. He had been furious then, and they'd temporarily broken up over it. But in time he had realized that her dancing was every bit as important to her as the prom was to him, and they had been able to compromise.

"You're absolutely right, of course," Fiona whispered. "Though it's easier said than done. Thank you, Jeremy. Do you know you're the best brother a girl could ever hope to have?"

"Of course I know that," Jeremy said, beaming broadly. Fiona threw her arms around his neck and gave him a fierce and grateful hug.

* * *

She telephoned Jonathan as soon as she returned to the house.

"I know you're knee-deep in calculus, but we have to talk, Jonathan," she said firmly, trying to keep the quiver out of her voice. "Please, will you come over right away?"

Jonathan hesitated for only a moment. "This sounds serious."

"It is. Believe me, it is."

"Okay. I'll be right there."

When he arrived, Fiona jumped up from the front step where she'd been waiting for him and ran down the walk to his car. They drove straight to Rosemont Park, their favorite place for walking and talking. The park was somewhat cold on this December evening, but it was as beautiful as ever. Four swans that must have forgotten to fly south were swimming in silent circles, looking like white ghosts on the black water. Even the bare branches of forsythia and lilac had a graceful winter beauty that gave a different light and shadow to the terraced paths.

Fiona's heart felt as cold and as bare as the branches. She looked up at Jonathan and thought sadly of how happy they had been only hours before. Now she had this painful news to tell him, and soon they'd both be miserable. Why did life have to be like this? Why?

She took a deep breath, preparing to speak. She had a terrible chore to do, and there was no way to make it any easier. So she might just as well come right out with it.

"Jonathan," she said as they walked around a

bend of the lake and stood near a bare weeping willow. "Something has happened. I . . . I received a letter today. . . ."

Jonathan stopped walking. He stood absolutely still, his gray eyes resting on Fiona's face. It broke her heart to think that he wouldn't always be just this close.

"I'd better say this quickly, before I lose my nerve." Fiona could feel beads of perspiration forming across her brow. "Jonathan, I've been accepted into the National Ballet Company. I received the notification today. They want me to be there by January first."

Jonathan didn't say a word for a moment. He simply stared at her, looking puzzled and sad. Then finally it seemed to become clear to him.

"You mean you have to go live in London?"

She nodded. Tears were running down her cheeks now, and she couldn't bring herself to look into Jonathan's eyes.

"I'm sorry," she whispered. "I wish I could stay here and things could go on just the way they've been. But I can't turn down the opportunity. It's what I've always wanted, after all. . . ."

"Oh, Fiona." Jonathan quieted her with a soft kiss. "I know," he whispered, wrapping his arms around her. "Of course you can't turn it down. It will be wonderful for you. I'm so proud of you, even though I'm torn apart at the thought of you going away."

Surprised, she tilted her head to look up at Jonathan. She couldn't believe he had said those encouraging words. But his face looked utterly sincere. His eyes, though sorrowful, showed that

21

he genuinely meant what he was saying. He *was* proud of her. And he knew that she had to go.

"Oh, Jonathan, I'm so happy you feel that way," she murmured. "I was so afraid you'd — "

"I'd what?" His face looked almost wounded. "Of course I'm proud of you. I know how important your dancing is to you. I'd never make that mistake again."

"Oh, Jonathan, I love you so much. What am I going to do without you?"

Suddenly Fiona began openly sobbing. It might have been easier if Jonathan had ranted and raved and gotten angry about her decision. Then they might have argued, and she wouldn't be feeling such pangs of guilt and sadness. But instead he had to prove that he was the most understanding, wonderful boy in the world.

"I'm going to miss you so much," she whispered as the tears streamed down her cheeks. "I'll never find anyone to love as much as I love you, Jonathan."

"Shhh . . . don't say that, Fiona." He held a gentle finger to her lips to silence her, then lowered his mouth over hers.

Fiona shivered, but felt Jonathan's strong arms grow tighter around her as she responded passionately to his kiss. She wanted to cling to this short, precious time, lock it forever in her memory so that when she was in London, Jonathan would still be with her in some way. She tightened her arms around his neck as if she would never let go.

But she knew that she had to let go. As soon as December was over, they would both have to let go.

Chapter
3

MEETING TODAY! proclaimed the sign on the seniors' special bulletin board outside the guidance office. Elise stopped on the way to her locker to read it.

SENIORS! COME AND HELP US PLAN A FORMAL HOLIDAY DANCE, the sign went on. THREE P.M. IN THE STUDENT ACTIVITIES ROOM.

"You're going, aren't you?" Emily asked, coming up beside Elise. "Let's hurry up or we'll be late."

"I had forgotten it was today," Elise admitted, "but sure, I wouldn't miss a meeting like that."

"Well, I have to miss a newspaper staff meeting," Emily said, "but I want to be part of this." The two girls walked together toward the student activities room.

When they got there they found it already packed with people, and they were barely able to squeeze in and find seats along the back wall.

23

"You're just in time," Diana Einerson called out to them. "Jonathan is about to bring this illustrious gathering to order."

Elise settled in beside her friends Dee Patterson and Marc Harrison and listened as Jonathan told how a large proportion of the class was interested in having a holiday dance. They'd have to do a lot of fast planning, but if they all worked on it, he was sure they could pull it off. As soon as he'd stopped talking, Elise raised her hand.

"I'd like to make a proposal," she began.

"We already know," Ben Forrest said with a groan. This brought hearty laughter and exaggerated moans from others in the class. "You want it to be a charity function, right?"

Elise grinned. "How did you guess? If we're going to dress up and dance and have a good time, why shouldn't the proceeds go to a good cause?"

"And I bet you know of just such a good cause," said Emily's boyfriend, Scott Phillips. He grinned at Elise.

"As a matter of fact, I do." Elise didn't mind that the whole class was teasing her. She was well known for being a do-gooder, but that was okay. She managed to accomplish quite a few worthwhile things with her reputation.

She went on. "The Children's Hospital is starting a building campaign this month. They're adding a whole new wing, and I think it would be great to donate a sum of money from Kennedy's senior class."

"Sounds good to me," Jonathan said. "Especially since we have a Kennedy student in Children's Hospital right now — football player Phil Carey. Anyone want any discussion about this, or shall we have a vote?"

A hand went up. Joel Kramer, a quiet senior who was seldom seen at class functions, stood up. "I have a suggestion from Adam Tanner, who couldn't be here today."

"Oh, yeah, Adam is probably out working on closing down that pet store," Jonathan said, nodding.

Elise froze. They were talking about Adam — *her* Adam. She didn't know his last name. Tanner. Adam Tanner. What a wonderful name.

"Well, Adam suggests that we give the proceeds of the dance to the Animal Rights League."

After that, a debate began, with people arguing the pros and cons of the hospital plan versus the animal rights plan. Elise was silent throughout. She felt that Adam's idea had merit, although, of course, she preferred her own idea. But it made her realize that her original assessment of Adam had been right. She knew when she first set eyes on him that they were on the same wavelength.

Jonathan called for a show of hands. The senior class voted for the hospital over animal rights.

"Tell Adam maybe our next charity function will be for the Animal Rights League," Jonathan said to Joel. "Now, we'll need a few committees to get this project rolling. Remember, we're working under some strict deadlines. We only have a couple of weeks to plan this. Elise, would you be willing to find a location for the dance?"

Elise nodded. "Sure, with Emily's help," she

said, looking toward her best friend. Emily nodded her assent.

Jonathan went on recruiting committee people until he had a sufficient number to help with the Christmas dance.

"Okay, looks to me as if everything's under control." Jonathan announced as the meeting came to a close. "Be sure to keep me informed, all you committee members, on what's happening. Next meeting will be on Thursday at three o'clock. See you all then."

"Right!" several voices called out.

Elise was jotting down the names of local hotels and restaurants as the room cleared out. She looked up from her notebook and saw that only a few of her closest friends remained.

"Jonathan, I just heard Fiona's big news," Dee said, moving to stand beside him.

"You did?" Jonathan said gloomily. He didn't look at all happy.

"What is it?" Elise asked. "I haven't seen Fiona all day. What's the news?" Fiona, a junior, had not been at the meeting.

Jonathan told them, in a dry, unemotional tone, what had happened.

"The National Ballet!" Emily exclaimed with a gasp. "That's terrific!"

"Atta girl, Fiona!" Marc called out. "Wow, some day she may be world-famous."

"We'll have to plan a going away party for her," Diana said. She began chattering about the party to Emily, Dee, and the others.

Jonathan turned away from his friends and busied himself gathering papers from the front desk. Elise put out a hand and touched his arm.

"But Fiona will be leaving Rose Hill for good," she said sympathetically. "Oh, Jonathan, this is so sad."

Jonathan didn't answer right away. He sat down behind a desk and looked up at Elise. And then he said in a very low voice, almost a whisper, "It's like a bad dream, Elise. I feel like I'm hanging on by my fingertips."

"Oh, Jonathan, I'm so sorry. . . ." Elise began.

"And the worst part of it is that I have to try to keep pretending that everything is all right," he went on. "I can't let these last few weeks with Fiona be miserable ones, can I?"

"No, I guess not," Elise said. "Every moment is precious, now."

He flashed her a thin, weak smile. "A guy has to be supportive of a woman's career, and that's what I'm trying to be. But it's hard, Elise, it's really hard."

"Well, let me know if there's anything I can do to help," Elise offered.

Jonathan gathered all his papers together in one quick sweep and tapped them together into a pile on the edge of the desk.

"Okay. I will. Thanks for letting me blow off steam, Elise," he said quietly, hurrying out of the room before anyone else could question him about Fiona.

"Thanks for getting me involved on your committee," Emily said sarcastically as she and Elise walked toward the office of *The Red and the Gold,* the school newspaper.

"Hey, come on. You don't really mind, do you?" Elise asked her friend. "It'll be fun, checking out hotels and restaurants."

"But I'm already so busy with my column and schoolwork and college applications — " Emily started to say. "Oh, there's my new friend from the newspaper office. I hope he went to the staff meeting."

Elise did a double take. Coming right toward them was Adam Tanner, the boy she hadn't been able to get out of her mind since the weekend. He looked even better than she remembered him: tall and sturdy and well dressed with the same stray curl tumbling over his forehead. His face widened into a grin when he saw the two girls.

"Hello there."

"Hi, Adam," Emily said. "Were you at *The Red and the Gold* meeting?"

"Yeah. There was lots of talk about your new column. Everyone loves it."

Although Adam was talking to Emily, he looked at Elise out of the corner of his eye. She felt the same surge of warmth rush through her body as she had the first time she saw him.

"Oh, thanks. I'm having fun doing it, but I still think the feature stories are much more important," Emily said modestly. So Adam worked on the paper. Of course. Elise had seen his name on by-lines!

"Did anything interesting come up at the meeting?" Emily asked. "We're just coming from the dance meeting and — "

Just then Scott Phillips, who was standing a few

feet away at his locker, called out, "Hey, guys. Can you come help me with something?"

Emily, Elise, and Adam all turned their attention to Scott, while a few boys, including Matt Jacobs, Marc Harrison, and Eric Shriver gathered around him.

"What would you guys suggest I do with a locker like this?" Scott asked with a sheepish twinkle in his eyes. He opened the locker door with a flourish.

Elise had to gasp at the gruesome sight. Scott's locker was jammed full with sports equipment, extra clothes, books, and utter junk — the accumulation of a whole semester.

"How could anyone I love be such a slob?" Emily demanded, letting out an exaggerated moan.

"Incredible," Elise put in, trying to keep her voice steady. She was beginning to feel dizzy, knowing that Adam Tanner had not taken his eyes off her since they met in the hallway. She hated this nervous, uneasy feeling. It wasn't like her at all. She always prided herself on being articulate, cool-headed, and self-composed. She just couldn't figure out her reaction to this guy.

"Well, Scott," she said, determined not to let Adam's presence affect her. "It looks like you need some help from someone who's organized. I'd say you should start by emptying out the whole thing and then — "

As she spoke she reached out and tugged at an old sneaker that was full of holes. She managed to pry it free, and suddenly every single item stuffed in Scott's locker came tumbling out. Elise jumped out of the way, but not before she'd been hit by a notebook, a pair of gym shorts, and a tennis ball.

"Way to go," Matt Jacobs cried out. A group of students stopped to stare, and Elise felt as if everyone was laughing at her. This was unbelievable. Once again she had totally humiliated herself in front of Adam Tanner, a guy she barely knew but might have liked to get to know better if she thought there was the slightest chance he would take her seriously. Well, she had nothing to worry about now. That very slim chance had just narrowed to no chance at all. Trying desperately not to burst out crying, Elise ran off down the hall taking refuge in the home ec room at the far end of the hall.

Once inside, Elise collapsed against a wall and sobbed out loud, tears of frustration pouring down her cheeks. How could she ever face Adam Tanner now?

"Elise . . . ." She heard Emily's voice with no surprise. She might have known her friend would follow her here.

"Hi, Em," Elise choked out. "Welcome to the Home Ec Emotional Comfort Center."

Emily bustled into the room, looking worried. "Elise, what's wrong? I've never seen you get so upset over a little accident before. I mean, you usually have such a great sense of humor. What's going on?"

"I guess I don't anymore!"

"Something must be bothering you," Emily insisted. "This isn't the cheerful Elise I know."

30

Elise sighed. "Okay, Em, what's the use of hiding it from you?" She turned around and faced her friend. "You're right. I developed a stupid crush on some guy, and it's been turning my life upside down."

Emily wrinkled her nose and studied her friend closely. "A crush? You? How come this is the first I'm hearing about it?"

"Because it's embarrassing. I made a fresh start as a newly independent person, remember? And then I met this guy, and it was sort of like getting run over by a Mack truck."

"A Mack truck, hmmm?" Emily said, smiling. "Well, I don't think it's any disgrace that you have a crush on someone. I think it's kind of predictable. You've always been a helpless romantic, Elise. I don't need to tell you that. And just deciding to change doesn't mean you really will."

"Well, this whole thing is humiliating," Elise said, twirling the heart-shaped locket she wore around her neck. "I don't want to tell you, or anyone else, who he is. I really wish I could just forget all about him."

"Why? Why not ask him out?" Emily asked. "You might be surprised. He'd probably be flattered to know that you like him. He'd — "

"No!" Elise practically shouted the word. "I don't want him to know anything about it. This crush is turning me into an airhead, Em. All I do lately is drop things and crash into things and act dumb!"

"Hmmm, I guess I see your point." Emily appeared to give the problem some thought. Finally she put out a hand and patted Elise's shoulder. "I do think I understand, Elise. And you know what? I think I may know the cure for you, too."

"Forget it, Em. There is no cure for this," Elise said in a flat tone. She felt a fresh wave of self-pity wash over her. She reached out and grabbed a potholder that hung from a peg on the wall. The cheerful hearts-and-flowers patterns annoyed her, and she flung it across the room.

"Elise, would you cut it out!" Emily's voice became sharp. "You're just feeling sorry for yourself. You know that won't do you any good. Anyway, I am going to fix you up with a fantastic boy who's going to make you forget all about this other guy."

"Oh, Emily, no," protested Elise. "I went on a blind date once, and I didn't like the feeling of going out with a total stranger. It's so . . . so awkward and so — "

"Elise, listen to me. It's the best way I can think of to cheer you up. And look at it this way. The holiday dance is in just a couple of weeks. Now that you're on the planning committee, wouldn't you like to have a date for it?"

Elise faltered. "Yes, sure. It would be nice, but. . ." She paused to consider what Emily had said. "Of course, there's no law against going alone, Em. I could do that."

"I know, but think about the possibility of going with someone special, someone to dance with, someone whose company I know you'd enjoy."

Someone like Adam Tanner, Elise thought. "Well, okay, Em. I guess it wouldn't hurt to meet this guy," she agreed. In fact, it was sounding better and better. She *did* need something to take her mind off of Adam Tanner.

"I mean it, Elise. This guy is great. He's cute, he's smart, and he doesn't have a date for the dance, either. He told me. I know the two of you will hit it off."

"Oh, yeah? Who is he, Rob Lowe?" Elise asked, almost forgetting to laugh.

Emily smiled. "I think I'll keep that a secret. For now. Let me work out the details with him, and then we'll arrange it with you, okay?"

"Come on, Em. Tell me who it is, pleeeease. Pretty please."

"I'm not saying another word. You'll find out soon enough. This is the perfect solution to your problems, Elise. I'm sure you'll go from being a klutz right back to your graceful self in no time."

"Do you think so?" Elise seized on that ray of hope and clung to it. "Good, I can't wait." She fumbled in her purse, looking for a tissue. "Thanks for being a wonderful friend, Em. I don't know what I'd do without you."

"You're welcome. Now come with me. I'm taking you to the girls' room to get cleaned up. You look terrible."

Elise tried to keep from laughing. "Watch it, Em. I could always change my mind, you know." But she knew that she wouldn't. She would go along with Emily's plan. She did want to go to the Christmas dance, and it would be kind of nice to have a date. She would just have to trust her friend and hope that sooner or later all thoughts of Adam Tanner would disappear.

Chapter 4

Elise sat tapping her fingers nervously on the table. It was Wednesday afternoon and she was in the Garden Room, a small, cozy restaurant in downtown Rose Hill. Overhead hung clay pots of green ferns, and between each table sat a tall potted palm. A gorgeous assortment of flowers grew in window boxes by the greenhouse glass walls.

The Garden Room was romantic, all right, and it had been specially chosen by Emily Stevens, incorrigible matchmaker. Elise smiled at the thought of her friend enjoying all the intrigue that went into setting up this blind date. "Can I get you anything, miss?" asked a slender waiter.

"Thank you, not yet," Elise replied. "I'm waiting for someone."

If only that someone would turn out to be a nice guy. Emily was right. It *would* be much nicer to have a date for the Christmas dance than to go alone.

Elise sighed and fingered the white carnation she had pinned to her blouse. It was a touch that Emily had insisted on: Both Elise and her blind date would be wearing white carnations. That was how they would recognize each other.

Elise glanced toward the door, wondering what her date would be like. She couldn't help hoping he might be a little like Adam Tanner, a boy who seemed so right for her. But she'd been avoiding Adam ever since the incident in the hallway at school the other day. Well, no use dwelling on that. She had to move forward, and maybe this blind date would be the start of something new and exciting. She really would give him — whoever he turned out to be — every chance in the world.

Elise kept her eye on the door, hoping to catch a glimpse of her date before he spotted her. She noticed that the door actually looked like the entrance to a real garden. It was surrounded by a trellis draped with vines and flowering plants. She was busy admiring some little purple flowers when she saw the boy with the white carnation. Her mouth fell open in disbelief. Her blind date was none other than Adam Tanner!

Elise almost choked. He walked in cheerfully, looking both excited and nervous. He looked so handsome in a hand-knit tan sweater that showed off his dark eyes and hair. His warm smile seemed to light up the restaurant the minute he stepped inside.

Suddenly Elise thought she might faint, she was so dizzy. She felt clammy all over. Everything blurred before her eyes, and all the sounds in the Garden Room seemed to amplify a hundred times over their normal volume.

Stop it! Stop it! she commanded herself. Pull yourself together. She tried to imagine what kind of advice levelheaded Emily would give her in this situation. "Whatever you do, don't panic," Emily would say. Good. Yes. That sounded simple. Breathe deeply. Don't panic.

I simply can't do it, she thought, feeling faint again. She looked across the room toward Adam. I can't go through with this. She couldn't have a blind date with Adam Tanner, a boy who turned her into a total wreck.

She could feel the tension building up inside her head, and she was sure butterflies were doing figure eights in her stomach. How could Emily have done this to her?

Adam spotted Elise and started toward her, his face lit up with a big smile. He was laughing at her, she was sure of it. And could she blame him? He must think by now that she was a total joke!

What can I do? she asked herself in desperation. The closer he came, the more panic-stricken she felt until she was nothing but a bundle of nerves and jitters that couldn't sit still.

Adam was crossing the room in long, easy strides, looking totally comfortable now. Elise's insides churned wildly. She did the only thing she could think of to do: She pulled off her carnation, smashed the flower into her purse, and quickly snapped it closed.

"Hi," Adam said in a deep, rich voice. His eyes twinkled with pleasure as he reached Elise's table. "Are you, by any chance, waiting for someone with a white carnation?"

"No," Elise blurted out before she could stop herself. "No, I'm not."

"No?" He looked confused. He turned slightly and surveyed the room, looking to see if any other girl sitting alone was wearing a carnation.

"But you. . . ." Adam stared at her, and she realized that he must have seen her stuff the flower in her purse. She could bear it no longer.

"I'm sorry," she managed to mumble, getting up from the table. Elise couldn't believe what she was about to do. But she couldn't help herself. It was as though she'd lost all control over her actions.

She bolted. She was out of the Garden Room and scurrying along Federal Street in what must have been record time.

Adam watched as the tall, dark-haired girl made her way between the palm trees and tables and vanished through the trellis. His mouth fell open in disbelief.

Is she kidding? he thought, running a hand through his hair. Or is she kind of crazy? Or maybe just the world's rudest girl?

Adam had seen her yank off her carnation. He hadn't imagined it. She looked up, turned totally pale when she saw him enter the restaurant, and then she'd whipped the flower into her purse. At first he'd thought she was playing a joke, but when she denied everything. . . .

Adam could hardly believe that *any* girl would do such a sneaky, cruel thing. But when it turned out to be that cute brunette from the mall, the one he'd been thinking about all week long — well, that made it all the more crazy.

He shook his head as if to clear it. He must be a terrible judge of character. He had felt certain the girl in the mall was someone special, someone he could relate to.

He thought of how excited he'd been when he walked into the Garden Room and saw her sitting there. He had thought it was an amazing and wonderful coincidence, because he'd been wanting to get to know this girl, anyway. He didn't enjoy blind dates, and the only reason he'd come was because Emily Stevens had coaxed and coaxed.

Maybe Emily would have some explanation of her friend's bizarre behavior. Adam hoped so, because he didn't have one clue.

Adam left the restaurant, got into his old blue Chevrolet, and drove straight over to Emily's house.

"Emily, I'm usually a very good-natured person," he said the instant she opened the front door.

She blinked in confusion to see Adam standing there.

"I know you are, Adam. That's why I fixed you up with my best friend. Where is she, anyway?"

"That's what I came here to ask you!" Adam pushed his way past Emily and stalked into her living room. "I must admit I'm pretty amazed about this whole thing."

"But what. . . ?" Emily closed the door gently, still looking confused. "Why are you mad at me? What happened?"

"Nothing, that's what happened." Adam's eyes blazed with anger. "The girl took one look at me and pulled off her carnation."

"No. That couldn't be true! I can't believe it." Emily's face turned a ghastly white. "Elise wouldn't do such a thing! She prides herself on being thoughtful and sensitive and considerate."

"And thrifty and wise and loyal?" Adam flung out sarcastically. "Well, forget it! She pretended she was never wearing a carnation and ran out of there as if the place were on fire."

Emily crossed the room and put a hand on Adam's arm. "I'm really sorry, Adam. There must have been some kind of mix-up. You're sure you noticed the right girl, with the right white carnation?"

"Emily, I'm not an idiot. I know how to spot a girl with a carnation. And I'm telling you, she pulled it off."

"No, it couldn't have been Elise," Emily insisted. "Elise has shoulder-length, curly brown hair; a cute, heart-shaped face; a big smile?"

Adam didn't have to hesitate for a moment. "The girl I approached is definitely a friend of yours. I've seen you with her. And she fits that description exactly."

"Well, this is very strange," Emily said. She

went to the bookcase and pulled out the Kennedy yearbook from the previous year. She flipped through the pages until she came to Elise's homeroom.

"Here," she said, pointing. "That's Elise Hammond, your blind date."

Adam stared at the picture, then turned to Emily with his eyes still angry. "Well, Emily, I've got news for you. That's the girl who told me she was not waiting for anyone, and then walked out of the restaurant as though I were a monster!"

Elise trudged along the avenue through a cold December drizzle, practically oblivious to the rain sloshing over her, soaking her through, and making her hair unbelievably frizzy. She knew she looked awful, but she didn't care. She felt awful, too.

This time, she knew, she had done the ultimate stupid thing of all time. She'd been rude and immature and impulsive. She had ruined her chances with Adam Tanner forever. And she couldn't be sure that Emily would forgive her, either.

She shivered from the cold and let out a miserable moan. How could she have done such a thing, lying like that, and hurrying away so rudely? Adam was bound to find out she really was his blind date, and then what would she do? He would never, ever think of Elise Hammond as a normal human being.

She passed the sub shop, a favorite hang-out of the Kennedy crowd, and considered going inside.

She could hear the animated voices of some of
the gang in there. She sighed. It would be so nice,
she thought, to go in and sit with her friends for
a while, maybe forget what she had just done.
Warm up, dry off, maybe have a bite to eat.

But no. On second thought she didn't feel like
seeing anyone, so she pushed onward. She couldn't
face anyone while she was in this mixed-up state.
Sniffling, she walked away from the warmth and
noise of the sub shop, and continued on her lonely
journey.

"I don't believe it," Emily kept saying to Adam.

"Well, you'd better believe it." Adam's face
was grim. "Your dear friend Elise Hammond is
either crazy or just downright cruel," Adam announced as he paced Emily's living room floor.
"She not only stood me up, but she actually looked
me over first, decided she didn't like my looks, and
then she walked out."

"Elise wouldn't do such a mean thing, Adam."

"I saw what I saw. The girl you just showed me
a picture of, the girl named Elise Hammond, took
the carnation and jammed it into her purse."

"Well, I don't understand it," Emily said. "She's
always so polite. She's known for being the most
kind-hearted girl in the senior class."

"That's a laugh," Adam said, folding his arms
across his chest. "Well, look, Em, don't feel bad.
None of this is your fault. You tried to make a
match that didn't work out, that's all." He started
toward the door.

"Adam, wait a minute." Emily looked worried. "Aren't you going to give me a chance to talk to Elise and hear her explanation? I know there must be a good one."

Adam hesitated for a moment. Then he looked at Emily regretfully. "I'd just as soon forget about the whole thing. I'll see you around," he said as cheerfully as he could manage. He stomped out into the cold rain and found it refreshing, as though it could cleanse him of all his conflicting emotions.

Elise Hammond. So that was her name.

As he drove home, he shook his head with disappointment. It might have been perfect, if only today had never happened.

Elise could hear the telephone ringing even before she reached her house. She knew somehow that it was Emily calling, so she didn't make any effort to rush inside.

She stood out on the front lawn, looking around at Everett Street and wishing that she were a little kid again. Everything was so easy back then. No formal dances, no blind dates, no embarrassing moments.

But even wrapped up in these fantasies as she was, the rain finally began to get to her. She was wet to the skin. Sighing deeply, she took her key and opened the front door. The phone was still ringing insistently.

She crossed the hallway to answer the phone in the kitchen, leaving a trail of puddles behind her. "Hello?"

"Elise. This is Emily. I'm calling for an explanation."

Elise took a deep breath. What could she possibly say?

"Oh, Em, I'm really sorry. I acted like a total jerk, and now he must be positive that I am one."

There was a moment of silence. "Elise, that's not what he thinks at all," Emily said. "Adam thinks you walked out on him because you don't like his looks or his clothes or something ridiculous like that."

"What?"

"You heard me. He feels rejected and insulted, and he's really upset. I don't blame him. Why on earth did you do it, anyway?"

"Oh, Emily." Elise tried to collect her thoughts as she combed her fingers through her tangled, damp hair. "It's just the opposite of what he thinks. Remember I said I had a crush on someone? A hopeless crush? Well, Adam Tanner was that boy!"

A gurgling sound came from Emily's end of the line. "You're kidding me."

"No, I'm totally serious. The problem is, every time I've ever seen him, I've done something stupid. Or klutzy, just like that day at Scott's locker. And I like him so much. That's the reason I couldn't face him today."

"But, Elise, that makes no sense at all."

"I know, but I couldn't just sit there and be his blind date when I'm so attracted to him . . . and after he's seen me make a fool of myself one too many times."

"You've had a crush on *Adam* all along? Well, then, this is a whole new ballgame," Emily said.

"I just know there's hope for you two. Can you come over here, by any chance?"

Elise let out a long, loud laugh. "I just walked a couple of miles in the pouring rain, and I'm not doing anything but getting into a hot bath. And what's more, there is no hope for Adam and me. I ruined all that this afternoon."

"Elise, don't say that. If we put our heads together we can — "

"Em, I love you, you're a terrific friend and really good at giving advice, most of the time," Elise said. "But this is one case where you're going to have to admit defeat. I could never face Adam Tanner again, not as long as I live."

"You're just being overly dramatic," Emily said. "There's always a possibility — "

"No, Em," Elise broke in sadly. "There is no possibility of this romance ever happening. Just forget it."

Chapter
5

It was a rainy Wednesday afternoon, and the members of the crowd were all jammed around their one special table at the sub shop. Fiona was practically misty-eyed as she watched Marc and Eric work their way through huge meatball subs, then focused her attention on Jonathan at the other end of the table as he led a discussion about bands versus disc jockeys for the holiday dance.

"So, Fiona, we're dying to hear about the life of a real ballet star," Diana said. "Tell us what it will really be like."

Fiona blushed and looked down at the table, then cleared her throat. She was pleased that her friends seemed to want to know about what her life would be like in England.

"First of all," Fiona said, "please don't call me a ballet star! I won't be that at all, not for many years, if ever. I'll be a member of the *corps de ballet*, the dancers who perform in a group."

"Like the chorus line in a Broadway show?" Dee asked.

"Well, yes, in a way." Fiona smiled. "And what can I tell you? I haven't been there yet, so I don't know much about it. My friend Lizzy tells me that life is very exciting for the ballet dancers because they're respected wherever they go. There's a lot of traveling, of course, and a lot of exhausting performances."

"Well, it all sounds very glamorous to me," Diana said with a sigh.

"Oh, it's not *all* glamorous, is it, Fi?" her brother Jeremy prompted. "There are some disadvantages, too, aren't there?"

"Of course," Fiona admitted. "It's a hard life. I don't deny that a dancer has to work very, very hard for her art."

"You're not kidding. You have to put up with bleeding feet and aspirin ointments and dancing twelve hours a day."

Fiona shifted uncomfortably at her brother's proclamation.

"Jeremy's not too far off," she said thoughtfully.

"Is the ballet life really that intense?" Dee asked.

"Yes, it is, especially in the National," Fiona said. "Even back in Kingsmont Academy when I was younger, each girl was totally dedicated to dance. We hardly knew what any other sort of life was like. We practiced all day long and never took a day off from dancing."

"But that sounds almost like torture," Dee said.

"It isn't, though." Fiona groped for words to explain. "It's simply the way ballet dancers are, and none of us thinks anything of it. For instance, Lizzy and I sometimes used to dream of sitting in a place just like this, a noisy, crowded fast-food spot, where tons of kids would gather to gossip, to talk about everything under the sun. It's true I won't have time to do this kind of thing anymore, but I've been lucky. I've been able to experience both worlds."

Fiona looked all around her and became lost in her reverie. She took in the details of the sub shop: the motorcycle on the wall, the Pepsi-Cola clock, the big stuffed bear, the antique jukebox, the Kennedy pennants flapping from the rafters. She wanted to impress each detail on her memory. She was going to miss this place. She had to blink to keep from crying.

"Fiona, are you all right?" Diana asked. "What is it? Are you afraid, sort of, to go back to that rigorous life?"

"No, no," Fiona managed to say. She fumbled in her purse for a packet of tissues. "I love the world of dance. It's what I want to be a part of more than anything."

"Then what's wrong?" Dee asked with concern.

Fiona looked around at the group with big, soulful eyes. "I'm going to miss all you guys so much," she admitted in a whisper. "It's going to be so difficult leaving here. . . ." She dabbed at her eyes with a tissue and looked down to the end of the long picnic table where Jonathan Preston sat, deep in conversation with Matt Jacobs. Fiona

47

watched the way his face muscles worked when he spoke. She saw the sharp intelligence in his soft gray eyes and the thoughtful tilt of his head when he paused to consider something that Matt had said.

Jonathan really was *perfect,* she thought. There would never be another boy like him anywhere.

"Well, we're going to miss you, too," Diana said softly. "Especially Jonathan. He's trying to be so brave."

"He's being absolutely wonderful," Fiona whispered. "That's what makes it so hard, Diana. I wish sometimes he'd get mad at me for leaving."

Just then Jonathan looked up and met Fiona's tearful gaze.

"Hey, looks like you're going to a funeral," Marc called out. "What are you all doing to make Fiona so unhappy?"

"I think Fiona is getting a case of the homesick blues before going away," Eric said. "What can we do to alleviate that?"

Matt Jacobs raised his root beer glass high above his head. "I think we should drink a toast — to Fiona Stone, who will one day be the prima ballerina who knocks England on its ear."

"And maybe the whole world," added Marc, also raising his soda. Everyone joined in the toast, shouting out jokes and trying to outdo each other. Now Fiona was sure she was going to lose it, burst out sobbing right in the middle of the sub shop.

Her eyes met Jonathan's again, and he instantly looked away. She noticed that he hadn't toasted her. As a matter of fact, he was being unusually quiet.

"To Fiona," Eric announced. "Someday she'll be a superstar. And let's hope she'll remember the clowns from Kennedy when she's at the top."

"Of course I'll remember you!" Fiona said, wiping tears from her cheeks. "Don't be ridiculous."

"I've got it," Marc announced. "How about if we make a pact right now? All of us will travel to England some day, en masse, to see Fiona dance. How does that sound?"

"Hear, hear!" Several of the boys approved this with solid thumps of their hands on the picnic table.

Still, Jonathan's gray eyes, looking downward, showed no emotion at all.

"Jonathan," said Matt heartily, giving his friend a poke in the ribs. "You're going to come with us to England, aren't you? We wouldn't want *you*, of all people, to miss the boat."

With all eyes on him, Jonathan was forced to produce a small smile. He looked up and finally met Fiona's gaze. They stared at each other like that, across the distance of the picnic table, for what seemed like a long while.

"Of course I'll be there to see Fiona dance," he said at last, and it sounded as though he meant it. "I wouldn't miss a trip like that for anything."

Fiona found herself breathing a bit more normally. Yet she knew, even though Jonathan had said all the right words, that he was not at ease.

49

He was desperately unhappy, just as she was, and with each passing day, their time together grew shorter.

Sorrow washed over her in great waves. Why was it, she wondered, that when you finally achieved your heart's desire, it had to cause such horrible torment? It just wasn't fair. There ought to be a way to avoid all this pain.

Chapter
6

Elise hung up the telephone.

"Well, that's it, Em," she said tiredly. "We've called every single hotel, and not one of them has an evening free for our dance."

"Except for that one we never heard of," Emily mused. "What was the name? The Lakeside?"

Elise stretched out her limbs and spine. She was stiff from sitting still for so long. She and Emily were making their calls from the Hammonds' den. They had long ago abandoned the chair and sofa and were stretched out on their stomachs on the thick beige carpet. Their task was beginning to seem hopeless.

"Uh-huh, the Lakeside Inn," Elise said. "It's way out in the boondocks, though, and it just re-opened after being closed for a couple of years. Doesn't sound like the ideal place to me."

"Well, the whole senior class is counting on us,"

Emily reminded Elise. "If we fail, there'll be a lot of disappointed people."

Elise shrugged. "Well, maybe we ought to check out this place then, take a ride out to see it. What have we got to lose?"

Emily nodded. "Good idea. We can go right now. Can we take your mom's car?"

"Sure." Both girls stood up and collected the hotel brochures and lists of area restaurants they'd been using for their search.

"Actually," Elise remarked, "now that I think of it, I *have* heard of the Lakeside Inn. I've heard my mother talk about it. I'm pretty sure they used to hold big, fancy dances in the early sixties. If it is the same place, she said it was fabulous."

Emily laughed. "Great, just what we need for our dance, an old sixties hangout," she said as she shrugged into her jacket and followed Elise out to the car.

Half an hour later, they found themselves driving along a winding country road on the outskirts of Rose Hill. The area was surprisingly secluded. There wasn't a housing development or an office complex in sight. A tunnel of hemlock trees surrounded the quiet, untraveled road.

"Spooksville, huh?" Emily kidded.

"Not at all. I like it out here. It's beautiful."

Both of them gasped when they rounded a curve in the road and caught their first glimpse of the Lakeside Inn.

"Why, it's . . . it's lovely." Elise spoke first.

"It seems to be." Emily was more skeptical. The big stone building that sat on a long, tree-lined knoll was certainly old. But it was also stately, with a porch running the whole length of it and ribbons of dark green ivy winding their way from the stone foundation to the graceful turrets rising on either side of the building.

And most impressive of all was the lake. Lake Hemlock wasn't very big, but it was clear and sparkling in the late afternoon light. Its borders were shaded by impressive maples and evergreens, and it looked like a picture-perfect setting for a holiday dance.

"Oh, Em, can you imagine how beautiful it would be here in the snow?" Elise asked, overcome with wistful, romantic feelings. She knew she was asking for teasing from sensible Emily.

But Emily surprised her by whispering, "Yes." She was obviously just as enchanted by the Lakeside Inn as Elise was. There was definitely something magical about this place.

"I hate to say this prematurely," Emily admitted, "but I think we've found our place!"

After the Inn's manager had shown the girls around, they were both in agreement: They had found the most romantic place possible for their formal dance.

"Even practical old Jonathan will love it," Elise said. "Everyone will." She and Emily were making the final decision while standing out on the side terrace, a rustic sort of patio that led off from the main ballroom where the dance would be held. Viewed from the terrace, the lake sparkled like a jewel.

"Right," Emily said. "Everyone will love it." She waltzed dreamily across the stone floor of the terrace to look down at the hillside.

Alone for a moment with her thoughts, Elise was overwhelmed with feelings that contradicted her recent declaration of independence. Did she really want to attend the dance alone? She had a wistful vision of herself dancing in the ballroom of the Lakeside Inn. She'd be wearing her green velvet dress, perhaps, the one that made her green eyes sparkle. Her hair would be dark and shining, and there would be tiny twinkling diamonds at her earlobes. . . .

. . . . And she'd be dancing with some really terrific guy, of course. Someone who could dance well, had a great sense of humor, and maybe even shared Elise's passion for causes.

Someone like Adam Tanner.

She shook her head and tried to clear it of this fantasy. No! Not only would she be attending the dance alone, but the chances were slim that Adam Tanner would even talk to her again, let alone dance with her.

A single tear slid down her cheek. Her dream had seemed so real for an instant. She could actually picture herself swirling around the dance floor in Adam's arms, under the soft glow of the holiday lights.

"Elise, are you thinking about Adam?"

"No." Elise shivered and rubbed her arms. The late afternoon air had turned cold. It even felt like it might snow. Elise exhaled and watched her breath form a little cloud and hang in the air.

"Tell me the truth, Elise. What's making you so sad? It is Adam, isn't it?"

"It doesn't matter."

"Yes, it does. Why are you being so stubborn? If you'd give me another chance to fix you up with Adam, you could just explain to him what happened, and everything could work out just fine, in time for the dance."

"No, Emily. Please stop bugging me about him."

"I can't help it. I hate to see you two not getting a chance to know each other because of a silly misunderstanding."

"Emily, if he was the last man on earth. . . ." Elise began. "Well, then maybe, uh. . . ."

"Yes?"

"Well, maybe *then* I'd be able to face him." She paused to consider this thought. "No, not even then. Forget it. I'll never ever talk to him again. And that's final."

Chapter
7

"Hey, lady," the little boy from Room 322 called out.

"My name is Elise," Elise said, smiling as she entered the child's room. She held out the clown puppet she wore on her right hand, made it do a little dance, and asked in a high voice, "What can we do for you?"

Elise always loved working at the Children's Hospital, but she was even more grateful than usual that she could take refuge here this afternoon. She wanted to be as far away as possible from Kennedy High, Emily, and anything that might make her think about Adam.

The little boy asked for a glass of water, and Elise had a feeling he'd only called her in because he was lonely. She chatted with him for a little while, let him try out her puppet, and had just gotten around to fluffing up his pillows when his mother arrived.

Elise smoothed her hospital jacket down over her hips, straightened her shoulders, and moved on to the next room and her next patient, Phil Carey, a Kennedy football player who'd been hurt in a game. He was a year younger than Elise, and she was pretty sure he had something of a crush on her. He paid a lot of attention to her, almost as though she were the patient needing care. And he insisted that she be the *only* volunteer assigned to take care of him. She was flattered by his interest, but that was as far as it went.

She knocked on the partially opened door.

"Come in," Phil called out. "Is that my personal volunteer?"

Elise walked in with a huge grin on her face. It was nice to be appreciated, and she always enjoyed her brief visits with Phil. "Hi, there, how are you doing today?" She headed for the window-sill to see if his plants needed water, then stopped short when she noticed Phil had a visitor. And not just any visitor!

It was *Adam Tanner*. He was leaning back against the wall by the big window, looking thoroughly relaxed. Just when she thought she'd never have to see him again!

"Elise," Phil said, sitting up in bed. "I don't know if you've ever met Adam Tanner. He's a reporter for *The Red and the Gold.* . . ."

"We have met," Elise said in a tight voice. "Sort of." She had to force herself to stay in the room. Her impulse was to flee in haste, not face him, talk to him, hear him. She didn't think she could bear it. Already she had a sickening sensation in the pit of her stomach.

Adam had smiled broadly when Elise first walked into the room, but his expression had quickly clouded over. Now he looked guarded and tense.

"Yes, we have met." His words came out cold and precise. "I don't believe I learned your name the last time, though."

Elise knew she had to do something, and it had to be something mature, for a change. She knew that an apology from her was in order.

Before she could let herself think about it, she stepped forward and extended her right hand to Adam.

"Well, please let me introduce myself now," she said clearly. "I'm Elise Hammond." She cringed when she heard how shaky her voice came out.

Adam looked startled, to say the least. He didn't accept her handshake right away. He stared at her in disbelief as if wondering if he should really take her seriously.

Bravely she moved forward, closer to Adam. "Look," she said. "I wish I could say that that girl in the Garden Room was my identical twin, Adam. That would solve all my problems."

The hint of a smile touched his lips.

"What's going on?" Phil asked, looking from one to the other from his bank of pillows.

"But the truth is," Elise went on, ignoring Phil, "that stupid girl was me. And I owe you an apology for what I did. I'm sorry."

"Amazing," Adam said softly, looking deep into her eyes. "You're full of surprises, aren't you, Elise Hammond?"

"I don't get it," Phil grumbled. "What are you two talking about?"

"We're just getting an apology out of the way, Phil," Elise finally explained.

Adam, still staring at Elise, said, "An explanation would be quite interesting, too, I imagine."

Elise coughed and tried to think of some way to change the subject. "Can't we shake hands and be — well, friends? Sort of?"

Adam grinned at that and put out his hand at last. "Friends," he repeated, sounding amused. "Sort of."

They shook hands. And that, Elise thought, should be the end of this mess.

But it wasn't, not by a long shot. As soon as Adam's big sturdy hand touched hers, she felt her spine start to tingle. She could feel the heat rising in her cheeks and her heart was pounding so wildly, she thought it might leap from her chest.

She tried to pull away from him, but he was holding fast to her hand. This only added to her confusion.

"Hey! I have something important to tell you, Elise," Phil called from his bed, trying to draw their attention back to him. He seemed unaware of the major undercurrents in the room. "Elise?"

"Yes." Elise gave a real tug and pulled her hand away from Adam's. She caught the look of surprise on Adam's face as she hurried around the hospital bed toward Phil.

"Guess what?" Phil said, looking excited. "Adam usually writes about important social issues, but this time he's here to write about *me*. Mainly about the important issue of injuries in high school football, but still, most of the article will be about me."

"That's great, Phil," Elise said, trying to sound calm. She refused to look over at Adam; she was intensely aware that his eyes were on her, watching her every movement.

"We were just discussing how many guys have gotten hurt on the football squad in the past few years," Phil told Elise. "Do you know how many times, Elise?"

"No, I have no idea," she said. "Listen, Phil, maybe I should come back later when you're not busy — "

"Oh, no," Phil protested. He grinned mischievously and gave Elise a pleading look. "I love having you here. And besides, I need all sorts of help. Ice water, another pillow, a bowl of ice cream."

Adam let out a laugh from the other side of the room. "I wouldn't let her too close with a bowl of ice cream. She might spill it all over you," he teased.

Elise didn't know whether to laugh or cry. It might sound like Adam was kidding, but she knew what he was thinking. She was a flake and an incredible klutz. She'd never be able to live that down!

Phil frowned at Adam's comment. "What are you talking about, man? Elise is perfect. She's never dropped anything in her life."

"Really?" Adam said with a devilish smile. "Not even a white carnation?"

Elise drew in a deep breath. Well, she deserved

it, but she could ignore it. She took Phil's pillow and gave it a ferocious whack.

"Don't leave, Elise. Stay here and keep me company. I really do need your help." Phil looked puzzled.

Elise sighed. She really was supposed to be here. But how could she stand to stick around with Adam studying her so closely?

She pummeled another one of Phil's pillows. She could get Phil his water and ice cream. That way she'd get a break from Adam Tanner for a while.

"You can go on with the interview," Phil said to Adam. "I'm sure Elise won't mind. Anyway, she might be impressed with my story."

"Oh, I'm sure she will," Adam said dryly. He took out his notebook and reached to pull a pencil from behind his ear. As he did so, his elbow slammed into a pile of schoolbooks resting near him on the windowsill. The books went flying and landed on the floor with a series of thuds.

Elise burst out laughing. At first she giggled to herself, trying to hide her amusement, muffling her laughter behind her hand. But then she could contain herself no longer and let out a long, happy laugh.

Phil laughed, too, but Adam turned a deep red and knelt down to begin picking up the books.

"Guess I'm not the only one," Elise couldn't resist saying.

"I guess not," Adam said sheepishly. He finally managed a small smile. "Sorry, Phil."

"No problem. Let's get back to the interview. Where were we?"

"Excuse me, Phil. Before you start, I just want to tell you I'll get that ice cream you wanted. I'll be back in a little while, okay? See you later." She paused by the door for a moment. "Er . . . 'bye, Adam," she called out.

" 'Bye, Elise," Adam said from his spot on the floor, where he was picking up the last stray paper. As he stood, she watched in absolute amazement as Adam bumped into Phil's hospital nightstand, nearly knocking over the vase of flowers that sat on top of it. Just in time, Phil reached out and kept the vase from crashing.

"Having trouble today, huh? I've never seen you like this before," Phil said.

On her way out of the room, Elise glanced back and noticed Adam still studying her. Again she felt that now-familiar shiver run up her spine. Well, he wasn't affecting her any less today than the first time she'd seen him. She really did have a hopeless crush.

Chapter
8

Saturday was a perfect afternoon for a football game. It was cold, but not unbearably so. Puffy white clouds moved across a pale blue sky. Out on the field, the Kennedy marching band was playing. Fiona, who had hated football when she first came to the United States, sat high in the bleachers, taking in the scene. She was wondering why today, everything about the game, even the brisk, cold weather, suddenly seemed extremely precious.

"Great game, huh?" Jonathan said with wild enthusiasm. He had one arm around Fiona and one arm high in the air, waving a Kennedy banner. Jonathan had always been a virtual nut about football and school spirit.

"Not bad," Fiona said quietly, and the funny part was that she meant it. She thought back to her disastrous first date with Jonathan. He had taken her to the Army/Navy football game, and she had been utterly miserable. She couldn't stand the roaring crowd, she couldn't understand the game, and she had been certain she would freeze to death. She had insisted Jonathan take her home before the game was over. Well, she'd come a long way since then. She still didn't love the game, but she had certainly grown to love Jonathan.

She settled back in her seat to enjoy the game. This might be the last American football game she'd ever go to, she thought sadly.

Fiona knotted her long woolen scarf and sighed, nuzzling closer to Jonathan. It wasn't going to be easy, leaving all this. Not just football, but everything she'd grown to love in the States. Kennedy High, all her new friends . . . and, of course, Jonathan.

She glanced up at him and felt a tightening inside her chest. He looked so wonderful. He wore his long, oversized gray coat with his ever-present felt hat, and his lean cheeks were ruddy from the wind. The bright red scarf around his neck accentuated his clear gray eyes.

If only she didn't love Jonathan so much, this wouldn't be so hard. But she did love him, more than she'd ever loved anyone. She jumped to her feet with the rest of the crowd when Kennedy scored, then snuggled into the warm spot under Jonathan's arm. She let out a cheer for Kennedy, grabbed Jonathan's banner, and waved it over her head.

"Hey," Jonathan said, looking down in surprise. "Am I imagining things? Is that my Fiona yelling about a touchdown?"

"It certainly is." Fiona flashed him a smile.

"Hmmm. Never thought I'd see the day," Jonathan mumbled. He scratched his head in exaggerated puzzlement. "Are you sure you're Fiona Stone? The British girl from Kingsmont Academy?"

Fiona laughed. "I'm sure," she said.

"Whoever you are, I love you," Jonathan said softly, bending down to whisper in her ear. She reached out and touched his cheek with great tenderness.

"I love you, too," she whispered.

She should be feeling so great, so lucky. She was loved by the most wonderful boy in the world. But at the moment all she could feel was a deep sadness, a torment almost, that reached right down into her very soul.

"Why, hello, Elise," said the school librarian, Mrs. Farnsworth, as Elise entered the library. "I haven't seen you here in a while."

"Hi, Mrs. Farnsworth," Elise said with a smile. "My schedule doesn't let me get in here as often as I'd like. But I'm here now to do a little research. I was hoping to see some. . . ." Elise lowered her voice and looked around to see if anyone was listening. "I'd like to see some back issues of *The Red and the Gold*," she whispered.

"You can get those in the newspaper office," Mrs. Farnsworth said, but Elise shook her head.

"Well, uh, I'd rather see your collection, if possible."

"Certainly. Follow me." The librarian led the way to a corner of the library. "They're kept over here."

"Thank you," Elise said quietly. She sat down at one of the round oak tables with a pile of newspapers in front of her. She fervently hoped that no one she knew would come into the library and catch her doing this.

She wanted to look at all the articles Adam Tanner had written in the past year.

She sighed deeply and began to thumb through the stack. She didn't have to look far. Adam seemed to have a story in almost every issue, many of them on the front page.

And Phil had been right; Adam almost always wrote about some burning issue.

HOMELESS OF THE CAPITAL NEED ASSISTANCE, was one of the headlines that called attention to an Adam Tanner feature. He'd written a terrific article on the Washington, D.C. street people and had included ideas about what could be done to solve some of the problems.

Another one was about Garfield House in Georgetown, where troubled teenagers and runaways received immediate help and counseling. And then there was a beautifully written piece, with photos, about the Animal Rights League and their fight to save unwanted puppies and kittens.

Elise stared at the growing stack of Adam Tanner articles in front of her on the library table.

Why, she wondered, had she never read these before? They were all about subjects that affected the community, things she was usually interested in. But she must have skipped right over these stories in favor of articles written by her friends. Why? Probably because the name Adam Tanner had meant nothing to her when the articles came out.

Elise rubbed her eyes and set the newspapers down with a discouraged thump. She thought back to the other day at the hospital, when she and Adam had shaken hands. She had been shocked at her own reaction to him. There had been such a physical impact, such an assault on her emotions, that she had felt odd and shaky the rest of that day. She had roamed around the hospital like a zombie after that handshake.

She hadn't seen Adam since then, but he'd been on her mind constantly. Elise wondered again if it was too late to patch things up with him. He really did seem perfect for her.

She looked up and saw Diana Einerson coming through the library door. Elise knew Diana would head right for her table as soon as she spotted her.

She didn't want to be caught reading all these Adam Tanner stories. She quickly put all the newspapers in a neat pile, scooped them up, and took them back to their place on the shelf. Then she turned and waved to Diana.

"Hi," Diana said, hurrying over to Elise's table. "How are you, Elise?"

"Good," Elise said with perfect control. "Just fine. What's new with you?"

"Well, two things: Holly and I are looking forward to a short trip to Montana over the holidays to see Bart and I found a terrific dress yesterday, on sale. You know, for the dance."

"Oh, great," Elise said, trying to sound enthusiastic. She still didn't know if she'd be attending. Some holiday season this was turning out to be.

"I heard that you and Emily found a really nice place for it," Diana continued. "Some inn that just reopened way out in the country?"

"Yes, the Lakeside Inn. Wait until you see it, Diana. It's absolutely beautiful . . . and very romantic."

"I can't wait," Diana said. Her soft blue eyes were brimming with eagerness. "Jeremy can't, either. There's something so special about holiday parties . . . remember last year when Bart and I had that party?"

"Yes," Elise said. She recalled that party well. It had been the start of her romance with Ben, her first boyfriend. She shook herself out of her reverie. "You've given some great parties at your house, Diana."

"Well, that brings me to the reason I came over here, Elise," Diana said. "Jeremy and I are planning a going-away party for Fiona."

"Oh, good!" Elise said. "When is it?"

"A week from this Saturday, at my house."

"Great! I'll be there."

"Be sure to keep it a secret from Fiona."

"Of course."

"Hey, Elise. Who are you going to the dance with?"

"Well, if I go at all, I think I'll be going alone."

"What?" Diana seemed shocked. "I thought Emily was fixing you up with some friend of hers."

Elise sighed. "Well, it didn't exactly work out, Diana."

"No?" Diana looked surprised. "I can't understand that. Any boy would be crazy not to like you, Elise. What happened? Didn't you like him?"

"No, that wasn't it," Elise said slowly. "I liked him all right, but . . . but there were some problems. It just didn't work out, that's all."

"Do you want to talk about it?" Diana asked.

"Not right now, Di. I have to get going. You probably came in here to study, and I only came to do some quick research — "

Elise was afraid she might burst out crying. She had to get out of there fast. What was the matter with her these days? She was like a bundle of loose nerve-endings. The slightest thing set her off.

She stood up and gathered her books. She wasn't ready to tell Diana or anyone else about Adam yet.

"I want to help out with Fiona's party, okay? I'll talk to you about it later."

Elise felt a rush of sadness washing over her as she left the library. That was just one more thing to make the holiday season crummy: Fiona would be leaving for England, and her friends might never see her again.

That night, Elise was surprised to get a call from Mrs. Phelps of the Animal Rights League.

"Hello, dear," Mrs. Phelps said. "You may not remember me, but I was at the mall during that protest against the pet store."

"Oh, yes," Elise said. She remembered her. "How did that turn out?" With all the confusion in each of her meetings with Adam since then, she'd never had a chance to ask him about it.

"We won," Mrs. Phelps said. "Once we had all that newspaper publicity, it was easy to get the store to close down."

"That's great," Elise said.

"Yes, isn't it? I'm calling you now because you gave me your name and phone number that day," Mrs. Phelps went on. "You said you were interested in helping us out if we were ever in need."

"Oh . . . yes, I am." As usual, Elise had over-committed herself. Between the hospital, planning the dance, and Fiona's party, did she have time for more volunteer work?

"Well, I have a project for you if you're still interested."

"I'd love to help," Elise said without a moment's hesitation. She'd find time. "I think the Animal Rights League is doing a lot of really great work. What kind of a project is it?"

As soon as Mrs. Phelps had explained the situation, Elise knew she had done the right thing. She couldn't wait to help out with a litter of new cuddly puppies.

And not only that. Somewhere in the back of her mind, a tiny thought was rattling around, telling her that she had another good reason to get involved with the Animal Rights League.

And that reason was named Adam Tanner.

Chapter 9

Adam was finishing up his latest feature article in *The Red and the Gold* office when Emily wandered in during her lunch period.

"Hi, there," she said cheerfully. "Are you still speaking to me these days?"

"Of course," he said, not looking up from his computer screen. "Why shouldn't I be?"

"Great." Emily put down a folder full of notes for her column. "I still feel terrible about the way things turned out with Elise. I wish I could talk you into giving her one more chance. . . ."

Adam turned sharply and looked her right in the eye. "Did Elise say she wanted another chance?" he asked eagerly.

"Uh. . . ." Emily knew she couldn't tell a lie. "Not in so many words, Adam, but I know she'd be glad if she could make it up to you. . . ."

"I seriously doubt that," Adam said, turning back to his screen.

"If only you knew her," Emily began. "You and she — "

"I do know her," Adam said. "At least, I'm getting to know her. We happened to meet yesterday at the Children's Hospital."

"You did?" This was news to Emily, who hadn't seen Elise yet today. "And you, uh, spoke to each other?"

Adam flashed Emily a dazzling smile. "Yes, well. . . ." He hesitated. "Of course, I might not have, after what she did to me, but she had the good sense to apologize."

"So you two are friends now?" Emily asked.

"Sure. We even shook hands on it," Adam said cheerfully.

"Great. Then maybe there's a chance that you two will go out again."

"Please don't start that all over. I know Elise isn't interested."

Emily didn't dare press the issue right then, but she knew Elise was interested. In fact, she had the very definite feeling that both Elise and Adam were interested, much more interested than either wanted anyone to know. She sat down at a nearby computer.

"I suppose you have a date for the dance by now," Emily said casually.

"No." He stopped typing for a moment. "I figure maybe I'll skip it completely. I have a few essays to write for my college applications, and I'm planning to knock those off during the holidays."

"All work and no play might turn Adam into a very dull boy," Emily said lightly.

"Yes, Dear Abby." Adam grinned at her. "My life is not all work. I'm going to be having some fun this afternoon. I have a project to do for the Animal Rights League that involves a whole litter of puppies."

"Sounds exciting," Emily said with a shrug.

She had no idea how prophetic her words were to be.

Elise guided her mother's car through a maze of traffic until she spotted a small sign that said Belvedere Street. She turned into a narrow street lined with huge Victorian houses with rambling lawns and old-fashioned gardens.

She was looking for number 85, the home of Ruth Clement. Mrs. Phelps had told her that Miss Clement, a volunteer with the Animal Rights League, was a foster mother to a new litter of puppies. The mother dog, a golden retriever cross, had been abandoned and picked up by the Animal Rights League. When it was evident that the dog was about to give birth, she had been taken in at Miss Clement's house. There she had delivered her puppies.

Miss Clement didn't drive, however, and the pups were due this afternoon at the animal clinic for their first shots. Elise had been contacted by Mrs. Phelps to help transport the newborns to the vet.

She could hardly wait to see them. She pulled up in front of what looked like one of the oldest homes on the block and hopped out of her car. An old blue Chevy was parked in Miss Clement's driveway.

Elise stood on the sagging old porch and tapped with the door knocker; there was no doorbell. She was busy looking at the gnarled vines in the big, overgrown garden to the left of the porch when the front door opened.

"*Elise*?" a voice asked in surprise.

"Hi, Adam," she burst out, unable to keep from smiling. "What are you doing here?"

"I work with the Animal Rights League, remember?" He opened the door wider and smiled back at her. "Are you coming in? I gather you're the fourth volunteer in this project."

"Yes," Elise said. "I guess I am."

Adam led the way through a long, dark hall into Miss Clement's dining room. Half of the room had been sealed off to provide a pen for the puppies. Elise squealed with delight at the sight of them — but there were so many! They were tiny puffs of golden-brown fur, tumbling and stumbling all over their mother, who seemed wonderfully patient and loving.

"Hello. You must be Elise," said Miss Clement, a small woman with a pleasant, round face. "Welcome to the doghouse. If you're wondering how many puppies we have, it's ten. And they're four weeks old."

"Ten! Wow, no wonder you needed so many people for this field trip."

The white-haired Miss Clement smiled and introduced everyone. "This is Adam Tanner, who came with his Chevrolet, and this is Kelly Marshall, who came along with Adam."

"Hello there," Kelly called out. She was a tiny girl, about fifteen, Elise guessed, with auburn hair, bright blue eyes, and freckles. With all the puppy commotion, Elise hadn't noticed her.

Was she Adam's girl friend? Elise wondered with a sinking feeling.

"Hi," Elise said brightly, trying to hide her disappointment. She had thought maybe she'd finally get a chance to know Adam better. This whole situation was awkward, to say the least. Adam, she thought, looked nervous, and he must have had good reason. Kelly was obviously his date, and he must have felt funny about seeing Elise with her.

Elise wished there was something she could say to put him at ease, but she couldn't think of a thing. Besides, she was feeling strong pangs of disappointment. Kelly Marshall was awfully pretty. And Adam was awfully cute. Of course, she must be his girl friend.

"Well, our appointment at the vet's is in half an hour," Miss Clement announced. "With two cars and four people, we ought to be able to accomplish this project."

They set up two cages, one in each car, and arranged to take five puppies in each cage.

"Is it okay if I ride with you, Elise?" Kelly asked shyly. "Miss Clement's going with Adam."

"Sure," Elise answered.

They scrambled to catch the wiggling puppies and calm their mother, who seemed nervous with the added commotion. Eventually they managed to get all ten into the two cars. Elise drove while Kelly twisted around in the seat to keep an eye on their five charges.

"These puppies are so adorable. I wonder what

happens to them when Miss Clement can't take care of them anymore? Can you imagine taking care of so many puppies at once? Miss Clement is incredibly generous."

"She is," Elise agreed, keeping her eyes on the road. "She must be a dedicated worker for Animal Rights. How about you? Have you been a volunteer for a long time?"

"Oh, me? No, I'm not in the organization." Kelly sat up in her seat and tucked a strand of hair behind her ear. "I'm a friend of Adam's. He asked me to come and help."

"Oh." Again Elise felt that sinking feeling as she wondered just how good a friend Kelly was.

Almost as if she guessed Elise's question, Kelly said, "Adam and I have been next-door neighbors practically forever. We live on Warwick."

Warwick Place was a quiet Rose Hill street about ten minutes from Everett Street. Elise remembered it as a wide avenue lined with spacious homes that could almost be called mansions.

"Warwick. Wow. I never would have thought. . . . But that old battered car of Adam's!" Elise burst out before she could stop herself. "It's such a wreck."

Kelly laughed. "Adam has always insisted on being independent. He doesn't like to take advantage of his parents' money. He prefers to earn his own way with summer jobs."

"Oh," Elise said thoughtfully. She really knew nothing about Adam Tanner, she realized.

"Yeah. He's definitely got a mind of his own. He plans to be a great newspaper reporter someday, writing stories that do a lot of good in the world." She turned to look out the window.

"I really admire him. Sometimes I can hardly believe that he's my boyfriend. I feel so lucky."

Elise almost choked. She tightened her grip on the steering wheel and swallowed to keep from exclaiming out loud. A sharp, stinging sensation spread through her body but she forced herself to smile and pretend that everything was fine.

Well, she reminded herself, she should have known. She had guessed it the moment she met Kelly.

As she drove along, she realized that it was best that she found out right away. Now that she knew Adam had a steady girl friend, she could forget him and stop mooning over him.

"I'm still getting used to the idea," Kelly went on. "I mean, we've been neighbors and friends for such a long time, but things were never romantic between us until just recently."

"Oh," Elise said, squirming in her seat. She wished the animal clinic were closer. She really didn't want to hear anything more from Kelly.

"Yeah, I was so surprised when Adam asked me to the holiday dance!" Kelly said gleefully.

"That's terrific," Elise muttered. She felt awful, as though she were about to explode into a million pieces. But there was a ray of hope; the trip was almost over. Up ahead she saw the sign for the animal clinic. She pulled the car into the parking lot and breathed a sigh of relief.

The waiting room of the clinic was packed with people and their pets, from the smallest cats to a huge Great Dane. It was mass confusion even before the group arrived with Miss Clement's puppies. Now it threatened to turn into a three-ring circus.

Miss Clement took a seat near the receptionist's desk, desperately trying to hold on to her two puppies. Kelly settled in next to Miss Clement and struggled with her own armload.

That left Elise and Adam standing side by side. Elise looked at him, then looked at the floor, then shifted from one foot to the other. Why did things have to be so awkward between them? She was feeling extremely uncomfortable, and she could tell that Adam was, too.

She headed for the only free chair left and sat down gratefully, relieved to be away from him. She couldn't get Kelly's story out of her mind. Friends *did* fall in love, as Elise well knew. After all, hadn't it happened to her and Ben Forrest last year?

The woman next to Elise was called into the vet's office, and Adam approached and sat down in the vacant seat. Immediately his three puppies tried to get into the box with Elise's puppies.

"This is insanity, isn't it?" Adam asked, smiling at her now. Elise couldn't help but smile back. She couldn't go on feeling disappointed and gloomy for long, not in this situation, surrounded by all these restless animals. It was really quite funny.

"Hey, watch out, there goes little Raccoon Eyes," Adam said, pointing to a puppy that was practically out of the box.

Elise giggled. "That's a perfect name for him,"

she said, putting the puppy back down. Just then one of her other pups leaped out of the box and took off for the far side of the office. Elise thrust her boxful of puppies onto Adam's lap and scrambled after it. Quickly scooping the puppy into her arms, she returned to her seat and gently set it down in the box, then took the box back from Adam, careful not to brush his fingers with her own. She didn't think she could survive another incident like the one in the hospital, where she'd felt such strong electricity when they touched. After all, Adam had a new girl friend. Elise was history. She had missed her chance, and he was obviously not someone who waited around for a girl friend. She knew that. All she had to do now was make herself accept it.

Chapter
10

Finally their turn came. Dr. Howard, the vet, came out of his office to welcome Miss Clement and her foster puppies. "We have a full house today, I see," he joked.

He took the pups two at a time for their first vaccination shots. Even with all the assistants that worked at the Animal Clinic, including Kennedy senior, Amy Atkinson, Miss Clement's puppies were a handful. Eilse had never seen such chaos.

After each shot, Dr. Howard mentioned that the puppies would have to be brought back in about four weeks for booster shots. That started Elise thinking about the future. She wouldn't mind volunteering to drive the puppies here for their next shots. She'd love to see them again in a few weeks. She did hope, however, that Adam wouldn't be a volunteer then. The less she saw of him, the better.

It was past six when they had all the puppies back in their pen at Miss Clement's house.

"Thank you, thank you all," the beaming Miss Clement said. "You have truly done a good deed today. How about some hot chocolate or a soda?"

"Sure, a Coke would be great if you have it," said Kelly.

"Nothing for me, thanks," Elise said. "It's getting dark and it looks like snow. I think I'd better head home, Miss Clement."

"All right then, dear. Come back and visit me and the puppies anytime," she said. Elise promised that she would.

She went out the front door and stood on the porch for a moment, watching the first flakes of the winter's first snowfall settle silently on the brick path that led to the street.

"It's beautiful, isn't it?" A soft voice came from behind a big bush in Miss Clement's garden.

"Oh," Elise murmured, her heart racing. "I didn't know you were out here, Adam." The wind whipped his scarf around and there were snowflakes on his cheeks and eyelashes.

"I'm sorry. I didn't mean to scare you." Elise felt herself go weak in the knees just at the sound of his voice. What was he doing out here? Why was he haunting her like this?

"Well, that was quite an afternoon, wasn't it?" she ventured.

"It was a lot of fun," Adam said. "Now that it's all over, that is." They both laughed.

Taking deep breaths to calm herself, Elise tried to stop her heart from hammering. She wondered if Adam could hear it. It was so quiet out here.

"I'm glad we had this chance to do a project together," Adam said. "Emily keeps telling me that you and I ought to get together."

Elise laughed again. "That Emily. I adore her, but sometimes I wish she wouldn't take her Dear Abby reputation so seriously."

The snow was coming down harder now. Thick clumps of sparkling white flakes clung to the bare branches and the tangled vines in the garden. The whole yard was quickly turning white, and Elise was painfully aware of Adam standing close by, close enough to touch.

His dark hair was partially illuminated by lights that glowed from the corner of Belvedere Street. Shadows flickered across his handsome face, then disappeared as the wind sighed through nearby pine trees. He moved a step or two closer to her.

Elise caught her breath. She didn't understand. Adam should have been inside the house with Kelly, and instead he was here, covered with snow, smiling at her, moving closer.

"I've got to leave now," she said in a big rush, putting on her mittens. "I don't like to drive in the snow. I — "

Before she could finish her sentence, Adam moved one step nearer and took her chin in his hand.

"Elise, you're a puzzle to me," he said. "I wish I could understand — " He stopped short and leaned over to kiss her.

He grazed her lips gently with a feather-light touch that sent her pulse soaring.

Why was he doing this?

Elise put up her hand to push him away, but both her hands found a resting place against his chest.

"Adam, are you crazy?" she whispered.

He seemed to hesitate for a moment, but then he was leaning back over her to claim a real kiss.

Elise let out a small gasp of delight just as his mouth closed over hers, filling her with a sudden warmth there in the cold, dark garden. She felt as though she had been waiting all her life for this kiss.

And it didn't matter, for this one moment, that Adam was in love with someone else. The only thing that mattered to Elise was that she was in his arms right now, and everything about this kiss felt so right. Her hands moved up around his neck, and she sighed in contentment.

A wind from the north howled around them, blowing snow from the bushes and dusting it across their faces. But the onslaught didn't dampen their kiss. They held each other tightly, clinging to this brief, magical moment. Elise couldn't remember anything ever feeling so right.

Suddenly she snapped back to her senses.

"No! Stop it!" she gasped, pulling away firmly.

He looked at her with a puzzled, pained expression, his dark eyes flashing gold in the light of the streetlamp.

"What's the matter?" he asked.

"Everything," Elise said, biting her lip to keep from crying. She was trembling all over. "You ought to know! You — you — "

"Adam! Hey, Adam, are you out there? Did you forget about me?" Kelly came clattering out onto Miss Clement's porch, shouting out into the darkness.

"No, Kelly," Adam answered in a distracted, husky voice. He was still staring at Elise.

"Wow, it's really snowing hard. We'd better get going," Kelly chattered. "Where are you, anyway?"

Elise was glad she didn't have to say anything. She felt indignation rising inside of her, choking her. She was too furious at Adam to trust herself to speak.

She tore out of Adam's arms and rushed toward her car, blinded by tears.

Adam stood motionless, looking after Elise, unable to believe that she had run off that way. What was the matter with her? Hadn't she felt the same sparks of electricity he had? The snow pelted his face, and the wind ruffled his hair as he stared blankly into the garden. Finally he saw Elise's car pulling away, and he knew she'd really gone.

"What was that all about?" Kelly asked, coming up behind him.

"Nothing," he said slowly.

"Come on, Adam. You can tell me. Do you like her? It looked to me like you two were kissing."

"Don't be stupid, squirt. You always did have the most active imagination in all of Rose Hill."

"So? That's why you like me so much," Kelly quipped.

"Hah. Sometimes I don't like you at all," he said, punching her shoulder playfully. Kelly was like the silly little sister he'd never had, and he couldn't resist teasing her.

"Why don't you like me?" She was doing her pouting act.

"You make up too many crazy stories. I never know what you'll be saying next. You ought to be a writer, Kel."

"Oh, Adam," she said, slipping her hand in the crook of his elbow, "one of these days you'll wake up and realize that you can't get along without me."

But Adam was no longer listening to Kelly's lighthearted chatter. His thoughts drifted back to Elise, and he wondered why she ran off like that. What could possibly have upset her so much?

He reached out with his free hand and swiped angrily at a maple tree. Rats. Everything had been going along so well. They'd shared this great afternoon together, and then that terrific kiss. . . .

Adam had just been about to ask Elise if she'd go out with him. He didn't think he'd ever liked a girl as much as he liked Elise, in spite of all the wacky things she had done. He had been thinking of her since the moment he first laid eyes on her during the Animal Rights League protest. But why was she always running away from him? Did she find him so repulsive?

"Ground control to Adam," Kelly called into his ear. "Are you there, Adam?"

"Yes," he growled, trying to shake all thoughts

of Elise. "Let's go say good-bye to Miss Clement. Then maybe I'll buy you a cheeseburger, squirt."

"Oh, goody." Kelly did a little dance. "Elise gets kisses and I get cheeseburgers. How did I get so lucky?"

Chapter
11

Elise drove toward home with snow slapping at her windshield and tears stinging her eyes.

The nerve of Adam, kissing her like that when he already had a girl friend! Just when she'd been thinking what a nice guy he was, he turned around and proved himself to be a creep.

Elise sniffled. No. Somehow she couldn't quite believe that Adam Tanner was really a creep. But she still had no explanation for why he'd kissed her in the garden just now. And on top of that, she had no explanation for why she reacted so strongly to him.

In spite of that kiss, in spite of his having Kelly as his girl friend, and in spite of all the problems that had developed between them, Elise knew that she was absolutely crazy about Adam Tanner. But she had to force herself to forget him.

"I hope I never set eyes on him again!" she said out loud as she pulled to a stop by a red light.

"I hope you never do, either," a voice said at her left shoulder. Elise turned, startled, and saw Fiona Stone all bundled up in a down jacket, scarf, and hat, smiling at her from the curb at the intersection. She was weighted down with her bookbag and dance bag.

"Oh, am I glad to see you, Fiona," Elise blurted out. "Can I give you a ride home? I could really use some company."

"Sure. I'd love a ride." Fiona was climbing in the door in a wink. "And you can also tell me why you're talking to yourself, Elise."

Elise tried to smile, but she couldn't quite manage it. Her face was streaked with tears, and she was finding it hard to drive. Finally, she pulled the car over in front of a block of stores.

There, multicolored lights from half a dozen Christmas trees blinked at the two girls in the front seat. The reminder of the holiday season made Elise begin crying all over again.

"Why, Elise, you're not only talking to yourself," Fiona said in alarm, "but you're crying! Do tell me what's wrong."

"It's so stupid," Elise said, dabbing at her cheeks with a tissue. "It's so stupid of me. All I need to do is forget about the boy, and then I'll stop making myself miserable."

Fiona's eyebrows went up. "Oh, really? Well, I guess you've got it all figured out. You don't need any advice, then?"

Elise choked on an attempted chuckle. "I'm sorry, Fiona. I suppose I don't need advice, but I do need a shoulder to cry on."

"Cry away," Fiona said, pointing to her own

slender shoulder. "What's going on, Elise? You've been rather secretive lately, and none of us has known why. We never guessed that there was some special boy in your life."

"He hasn't exactly been *in* my life, but he hasn't been out of it, either." Right away Elise knew that that was a ridiculous statement. She took a deep breath and tried to explain to Fiona. She told her about Adam Tanner, from their first meeting in the mall, up to that absolutely wonderful kiss they had just shared.

"My word," Fiona said in her clipped British accent. "He kissed you like *that* and his girl friend was only a few feet away? Makes him sound rather like a cad."

"I know." Elise started crying again. "But even so, I can't help it. I think I'm in love with him."

"Still, you never want to see him again," Fiona added. "You just said so a minute ago."

"Oh, I don't know, Fiona. I can't make up my mind." Elise managed to grin weakly at her friend. "But I am grateful to you for listening. It really does help to talk to a friend, you know."

"Of course. I do know." Fiona's small face seemed to have a faraway look all of a sudden, as though her mind had gone on to some other, more personal, thought. She stared out at the heavy snowfall as if it were the last one she'd ever see.

Elise became instantly aware of Fiona's preoccupation. "I know you have problems of your own, Fiona," she said. "Especially now during your last month here in the States."

In the light from the Christmas trees, Fiona's face took on a haunted look. She looked thinner than Elise had ever seen her, and her lean face seemed even more angular than usual.

"Don't let me get started on my woes, Elise," she said quietly. "We really don't want two of us crying at the same time, do we?"

Elise put out a hand to touch Fiona's arm. "It must be so hard for you. I can't imagine what it must feel like to be leaving Rose Hill. It's something I've never had to deal with."

"Well, all of you will be leaving next year for college," Fiona said, as tears sprang to her eyes. "But I imagine that will be different. Everyone in the crowd will be leaving after graduation. And you'll at least be staying in the States, where you can come home for holidays."

Poor Fiona, Elise thought with a pang, glad that Diana was busy planning a surprise party for her. Elise just hoped it was the best, liveliest party that Rose Hill ever saw.

"Oh, Fiona," Elise said. "I feel ashamed for crying over my stupid problem, when you — you have a bigger, more complicated, *real* problem."

"Hey. Everyone's problem is real," Fiona said, obviously trying to sound brave. One tear trickled down her cheek.

"If only . . ." Fiona started to say.

"If only what?" Elise probed.

"If only . . . if only I didn't love Jonathan so much, all of this would be easier to bear." Fiona's voice cracked, and she covered her face in her hands. The shadows of the falling snow, together with the Christmas lights, sent eerie patterns flashing through the car's interior.

"But you do love him," Elise whispered. "And he loves you very much." She didn't mention what Jonathan had said to her in the student activities room — how he didn't want to make things any harder on Fiona.

"Yes. Unfortunately we do love each other. Sometimes I wish we didn't. It wouldn't be such agony to leave him then, Elise," Fiona said. "I never dreamed it would be so hard."

This time Elise said nothing. She just sat still and listened.

"You know the ballet *Swan Lake*?" Fiona said.

"Yes, of course."

"Well, there's a scene in the last act when Odette, the swan queen, dances out her grief, because she's going to lose her love, the prince." Fiona twisted in her seat to look at Elise. "Sometimes I feel like Odette, Elise. As though I'm dancing out my grief. . . ." Her tears came fast and hard then, and she wiped at her eyes with the backs of her hands.

Elise had never heard anything so sad in her life. She could think of no way to comfort Fiona, so she patted her hand and allowed silence to fill the car. Even the snowflakes settling against the car windows were quiet as a whisper.

The first snowfall of the season was so beautiful. Elise wished she could have enjoyed it more. Instead, she and Fiona sat, each wrapped in their own thoughts, pondering their misery.

"Fiona, the phone's for you," Jeremy called out later that night. "It's Jonathan."

"I've got a great idea," Jonathan said with enthusiasm as soon as Fiona picked up the phone. "Can we use the VCR at your house?"

"Sure, I guess so," Fiona said. "What for?"

"I've rented a movie for us," Jonathan said. "You've been looking so sad lately, and besides, we haven't had much time to be alone together. How about it?"

"Wonderful," Fiona said. "Are you going to tell me what movie?"

"That's the best part! It's one that you're going to love!"

"I'm dying of suspense, Jonathan. Tell me what it is."

"*The Nutcracker*. It's a ballet with Mikhail Baryshnikov, and I know you love — "

"How lovely," Fiona lied. She would never tell Jonathan that she had seen *The Nutcracker* at least ten times — not when he was doing this for her.

When he arrived at her house, no one was at home but Fiona. Jeremy was studying at Diana's house, and Mr. and Mrs. Stone had gone out to a concert in Washington.

Jonathan came into the living room and, still in his coat, swept Fiona up into his strong arms. His face was ruddy, his hair damp from the snow, and he smelled cold and outdoorsy. Fiona met his kiss and threw her arms around his neck.

"I love you, you know," she said in a tight voice. "No matter what, I do love you."

Jonathan put Fiona down and gently touched her cheek. "I know that, Fiona. I do." They melted together again for another kiss, longer and sweeter. But instead of Fiona's heart leaping with happiness, it seemed to be plummeting.

The pain just never goes away, she thought sadly, pulling away.

When they finally settled down to watch the film, they had a heaping bowl of popcorn on the table in front of them, a mountain of soft pillows behind them.

"I think I'm in heaven," Jonathan said with a sigh, putting his arm around Fiona and pulling her close.

Then why does it feel so awful? Fiona wondered. But she didn't say a word. She tried to concentrate on the movie, but spent at least half of it kissing Jonathan.

Once, surprised, she put out a finger and touched a wet spot on his cheek. "I thought American boys never cried," she said softly.

"I wonder why you thought that," Jonathan said, his voice subdued.

"Oh, Jonathan, I know exactly how you feel." Fiona kissed the spot where the tear had been. "I want to cry all the time, too."

"We have less than three weeks left," Jonathan said. "That time is going to go by like a shot."

"But don't forget, you're going to come to England to visit me." It was a brave attempt to sound lighthearted, but it failed. Fiona knew in her heart of hearts that very few, if any, of her Kennedy friends would ever venture over to England, even Jonathan. They were all saving their money for college.

"Yeah, we're all going to come and see you when you star in some fantastic show, like this

Nutcracker." He ran his forefinger sadly along the lines of her face.

"Maybe *Swan Lake*, who knows?"

"What's that?" Jonathan said, and she wondered if he was teasing her or not. How could anyone not know *Swan Lake*?

But of course, Jonathan was not a big ballet fan. He really knew very little of her world of dance. In fact, if Fiona were perfectly honest with herself, she would admit that she and Jonathan had very, very little in common.

She shook that thought away. She didn't want to think like that.

Jonathan was just reaching for her for another kiss when they heard the front door close.

"Howdy, folks," called out Jeremy, putting on his best American cowboy accent. "It's still snowing hard, so I came home early. Am I interrupting something, or can I come in and join you?"

Fiona saw Jonathan's shoulders slump with disappointment. He really wanted to be alone with her tonight.

But she heard herself saying, "No, come on down, Jeremy. You can watch the second half with us. Just don't try to steal all of our popcorn!"

Fiona knew that Jonathan was looking at her in puzzlement. She pretended not to notice it. She settled back among the sofa pillows and stretched out her long legs in front of her to get good and comfortable.

For some reason, she was glad that Jeremy had come home.

Chapter
12

"If you'll just clean it up a little bit each day, Scott, I'm sure you'll be surprised how easy it is to do. . . ."

Emily and Scott were standing in front of his now-infamous hall locker, and Emily was trying to convince him that a neat locker was worthwhile. She had to admit his locker now looked a lot better than it had a few days ago, anyway. After all the contents had fallen out on Elise's head, Scott had been too ashamed to revert completely to his old ways.

"For instance, look at this. I know you don't need this poster announcing a race that was held last June," Emily was saying. Just then Adam Tanner came ambling down the hall. His handsome face was a study in scowling.

"Hello, Adam," Emily said cheerfully.

"That friend of yours," Adam lashed out without even saying hello, "has *got* to be the most infuriating human being ever put on this planet!"

Emily's eyes widened with shock. "What? Are you talking about Elise?"

"I am," Adam said. His cheeks flushed an even deeper red beneath his normally ruddy complexion. He stood tall, looking indignantly at Emily.

"I thought you and Elise were friends now," Emily sputtered.

"Are you kidding? Any sort of normal relationship with that girl is impossible," he threw out as his parting shot. Then he walked off in a great huff.

Emily and Scott turned to stare at each other. "Uh-oh," Emily said. "What do you think could have happened?"

Scott shrugged, and they both turned their attention back to cleaning out the locker.

Minutes later Elise came along, walking alone in the tide of the hallway traffic.

"Elise," Emily said. "The oddest thing just happened. Adam Tanner — "

"Don't mention that name to me," Elise interrupted. "He has got to be the rudest, most exasperating boy who ever lived."

"Hmmm. Is that so?" Emily commented almost under her breath. "Would you like to expand on that observation?"

"No, I would not," Elise said, stuffing her hands in the oversized pockets of her bright red jumpsuit. Emily couldn't help but notice how unhappy her friend looked. Unhappy and angry.

Elise started to charge off down the hall, but

Emily ran after her, caught her arm, and spun her around.

"You're not going to tell me what happened with Adam?" Emily asked breathlessly. "I know something must have gone on."

Elise looked at her friend. "What did *he* say happened?"

"He didn't say. He was too busy being angry at the most infuriating girl on this planet — you."

Elise's green eyes flashed with anger. "I can't believe it! He had the nerve to say that about me?"

"Yes, Elise." Emily was beginning to find this whole thing amusing, although she tried not to let it show. "You each must have done something terrible to make the other so mad."

Elise took the bait, as Emily thought she would. "*He* did something terrible, Em, not me! Would you believe. . . ." Elise lowered her voice to a whisper, noticing passing students were beginning to stop and stare.

"Would you believe that he kissed me? Right on Miss Clement's porch!"

Emily's eyes popped open wide. "What? Adam kissed you? Who's Miss Clement? What are you talking about?"

Elise explained quickly because she had to hurry on to her Spanish lit class.

"So he's got this girl friend named Kelly," Elise finished, "and there she was, right behind us, calling out. 'Adam, did you forget about me?' Can you believe it? Isn't it outrageous?"

"Well, I have to admit this is a strange new development," Emily said when Elise had finished, still trying to keep from smiling.

"Don't start getting that matchmaker look in your eyes again, Emily," Elise warned. "He *has* a girl friend!"

When Elise had hurried off down the hall, Emily finally was able to let out her laughter. She went over to Scott and whispered into his ear, "Methinks they both protest too much, and me-also-thinks that there's hope for this love story yet."

Fiona loved ice-skating. She'd said yes immediately when Diana suggested that some of the crowd go skating at the Capitol Ice Rink that Friday night. She needed some extra exercise to burn off her restless energy.

Tonight the rink was crowded. It was bursting at the seams with chatter, shrieks, loud music, and brightly colored lights. It was a zoo, actually, but Fiona didn't care. She didn't often get the chance to be on her ice skates.

"You have really strong ankles, I take it," said Diana, looking down at Fiona's legs. Fiona was already making little circles with her blades while she waited for Jonathan to finish lacing up his skates.

"Of course she does," Jeremy told Diana with a laugh. "Not to mention strong leg muscles."

"Well, she's lucky," Diana said. "I'm not sure my ankles will hold me up."

There was a break in the music, and the four

of them decided it was time to plunge out into the rink traffic.

"This is scary," Diana howled, already slipping and sliding. Luckily Jeremy grabbed her and kept her from falling flat on her face.

"How about you, Preston? Are you any good on ice skates?" Ben Forrest came along from behind them, ready to tease Jonathan.

"I was born on ice skates," Jonathan bragged. Then, throwing caution to the winds, he tried a fancy turn while holding Fiona's hand. To her horror, Jonathan managed to pull both of them down on the ice.

"Born on skates, hmmm?" Ben looked gleeful as he helped Fiona up and left Jonathan sprawled on the ice.

"Thanks, Ben," Fiona said. She held out a hand to help Jonathan, annoyance mounting. She had been skating along just fine, and Jonathan had had to show off. He was such a ham sometimes, always wanting to be the center of attention.

"Hey," Jonathan said to her as they skated along smoothly now. "Did you get hurt, Fi? Why the sour face?"

"I just hate to fall, that's all," she said truthfully. "After all, a dancer spends her life trying to gain control over her body. It seems like the ultimate disgrace to flop down for any reason."

Jonathan pushed back his hat and narrowed his eyes. "You're not a professional dancer every hour of every day, are you? I mean, just for this occasion, can't you be plain old Fiona Stone?"

"It doesn't exactly work that way," Fiona said.

"A dancer is what she does. Don't you understand?"

"No, frankly." Jonathan's face clouded over. "A dancer is what she does. Sounds like some kind of propaganda you learn at ballet school. When you get to the National Ballet in London, does the real Fiona Stone cease to exist?"

Fiona pondered that as they skated along.

"Perhaps, in a way," she answered honestly. "One lives and eats and sleeps for ballet. It's all there is, a good percentage of the time. Real life does cease to exist in many aspects."

"Then I feel sorry for you, Fiona," Jonathan said gruffly.

Fiona decided it was time to drop the subject entirely. Of course he could never understand; no one could. She reached out for Jonathan's hand and shrugged.

"Let's just enjoy the skating," she suggested.

But a lot of little annoyances seemed to crop up that evening. Fiona couldn't figure out why everything Jonathan did seemed to rub her the wrong way.

She didn't like the way he monopolized the conversation at times, talking louder than anyone else. She didn't care for the way he skated, either. He was a decent skater but he was still determined to show off, and she was determined not to be pulled down by him again.

It was when they were at the refreshment stand that Fiona really felt irritated. She was sipping a diet soda while Jonathan was wolfing down two hot dogs with all the trimmings.

Suddenly she found herself staring at those hot

100

dogs. They were so American, and so, well, disgusting. She couldn't believe anyone could eat something dripping with sauerkraut, mustard, and onions.

"Want a bite?" Jonathan asked generously. She shook her head and tried to keep from shuddering with distaste. In England no one she knew would consume such an abomination.

She couldn't bear to watch him eat any longer. She turned away and stared out at the ice rink, her eyes blurring as she took in the speeding skaters and the blinking mirrored lights.

Her thoughts drifted to something her ballet teacher once said, something about dancers having to give up everything for their art.

It's true, Fiona thought. I do have to make many sacrifices for ballet. For Fiona, relinquishing everything and everyone in Rose Hill was just the beginning.

She leaned back against a pillar, her thoughts whirling around as fast as the skaters. She wondered why she felt so impatient with Jonathan tonight.

She breathed deeply and turned to Jonathan. "I think I'll meet you later," she said impulsively. "You just finish eating. I'd like to skate alone for a bit."

And she went off, feeling amazingly free and unhampered, whizzing across the ice like a graceful ballerina. She realized with relief that the recent, ever-present pain in her chest seemed to have lifted a little.

Later, when Jonathan drove her home, Fiona

was still feeling oddly detached from him and unbelievably lighthearted.

"Did you see who Ben Forrest was skating with?" Jonathan asked, pulling the car into the Stones' driveway. "He met up with some girl from another school, and they spent the whole evening together."

"That's nice," Fiona said automatically.

"Yeah, I think she's some kind of brain like he is. He met her originally at a science fair. Hey, Fiona, come over here. Why are you sitting so far away from me?"

"I dunno." She shrugged and snuggled in closer to Jonathan.

He bent over to kiss her.

"Oh, dear," she said in protest.

"What's wrong?"

"You smell like onions and sauerkraut," she said. "Not particularly romantic."

"Are you serious?" Jonathan asked, sounding shocked.

"Yes. It's a horrible American habit. You eat all sorts of junk and then try to be romantic."

Jonathan's face froze. Every muscle seemed to harden as he stared incredulously at Fiona.

Finally he spoke in a quiet tone. "Well, let's just forget it, then. We wouldn't want to offend the delicate British sensibility, would me?"

Fiona leaped out of the car before he could say anything else. She tore up the walk to the front door, wondering what ever had made her think Jonathan was perfect in the first place.

Chapter
13

Elise stood for a moment out in the freezing cold, staring up at the two huge brick buildings that made up the Rose Hill Children's Hospital. Today it looked like a rainbow at the end of the storm.

She was being melodramatic, she knew, but she was feeling a lot of turmoil. She had decided that keeping very busy was the only way to put the Adam Tanner incident behind her. And what better way to keep busy than to do lots of volunteer work at her favorite place?

After all, she'd done as much work as she could for the formal dance committee. After she and Emily had wrapped up the booking of the Lakeside Inn, Elise had worked long hours with the art students in designing posters for the dance. Then they had posted the signs all over school.

No doubt about it, the posters looked great, but Elise felt doubly dismal every time she saw one of them and pictured Adam Tanner, Kelly Marshall wrapped in his arms, spinning around the romantic terrace of the Lakeside Inn. Elise imagined herself off in a corner, watching all the dancing couples like some sort of chaperon.

As she trudged into the hospital building, she wondered what had happened to the independent Elise of several weeks ago. She knew she was still doing fine on her own, but the truth was, she couldn't get Adam Tanner out of her mind.

She worked so hard all afternoon, one of the nurses asked her what had happened to turn her into such a whirlwind today. She could have answered, "A broken heart," but thought better of it. Instead she quipped, "I ate my Wheaties this morning."

"Well, we've been hearing some great things about you, Elise," the nurse said with a big smile.

"You did?" Elise was surprised. "What?"

"We heard that you were singlehandedly the force behind this charity dance that the senior class is giving." Several of the nurses at the station nodded in approval. "This hospital is mighty grateful to you and your classmates, Elise. You've given our building fund a nice boost."

"I hardly did anything," Elise murmured, but inside she felt rather proud. Maybe she was unlucky in love, but at least she had done a good deed.

She had a surprise waiting for her when she got to Phil Carey's room.

"I've been waiting for you all day," the football player said in an excited voice. "I have something for you, Elise."

He was sitting up in bed, his leg freed of its cast, and he was holding a tall green paper cone full of long-stemmed white roses.

"These are for you," Phil said with a smile. "White roses for a pretty girl."

"Thank you, " she said. "But I don't understand. People are supposed to give you flowers when you're in the hospital."

"I'm going home soon," Phil said happily. "And I wanted to say thanks. The flowers are my thank-you gift."

"You didn't have to do that," Elise murmured as she accepted the beautiful bouquet and held it up to her nose. The fragrance was exquisite.

"Elise, I wanted to ask you to the dance," Phil suddenly confessed. "I know I'm a lowly junior, but I thought if you didn't already have a date, and if I was able to walk by then. . . ."

She stared at him with wide eyes. Maybe there *was* a Santa Claus, after all.

He went on. "But the thing is, my family is taking me away to Florida as soon as I get released."

"Oh." Elise's bubble burst at once.

"Yeah. The doctors think I can recuperate better in a warm climate. That's really a bummer, isn't it?"

Elise tried to compose herself before answering. She had to struggle to hide her disappointment. "It'll be good for you, Phil. Warm weather and strong sunshine sound like great medicines to me."

"Nah." He reached out and tried to grab her hand. "It would have been better medicine to be with you at the dance."

She smiled. "Well, it was a nice thought, anyway."

Just as well, Elise thought. She already felt like Phil's older sister as it was. If he was on crutches and couldn't dance, and she didn't really care for him romantically, the whole evening might have been a total washout.

Still, she'd been excited for a minute about having a date for the dance.

She helped Phil take a stroll down the hospital corridor, still holding her roses as she walked slowly beside Phil on his crutches.

"I can't go too far from my room," Phil said as they passed the nurses' central desk. "I'm expecting company today. Adam Tanner is coming back to finish up that football interview."

"*Today*?" Elise squealed.

"Uh-huh. He has a few more questions to ask."

"Listen, you're going back to your room," Elise blurted out. "I've got to get out of here. Come on, Phil, let's turn around and get back — "

"Why? What's wrong, Elise?" He looked shocked that the usually gentle Elise was now attempting to hurry him along in the opposite direction.

"Please," she said. "I can't be here when he — "

But it was already too late. Elise watched with a sinking heart as the elevator door opened at the end of the hall.

Just as she had feared. She had no personal Santa Claus or fairy godmother looking out for her. Adam Tanner strode down the hall toward them. He looked terrific, as always. He also looked mildly surprised to see Elise in the hall.

She groaned inwardly. She couldn't just leave Phil there on his crutches and duck into some other room. She was completely trapped!

"Hi, Adam," Phil greeted. "You remember Elise from last time."

Adam nodded his head but said nothing.

"How do you like the roses I gave Elise?" Phil asked. Adam's eyes flickered to the flowers in Elise's arms. Phil went on, "We've been talking about going to the Christmas dance together. . . ."

"Oh, really." Now Adam looked straight at Elise. She could feel the blood rushing to her face. She was afraid she was going to fall apart, but instead she stood up as straight as she could and stuck out her chin.

Two could play at this game.

Still, only one image raced through Elise's mind, the image of those soft lips on her own. She had a hard time tearing her gaze away from Adam's mouth.

"It's nice to see you again, Elise," Adam said in a nonchalant, friendly way. "Usually whenever I see you, you're in the process of rushing away."

"Well, I . . ." she stammered, "as a matter of fact, I was just about to leave now. . . ."

"She said she had to get out of here before you arrived," Phil said helpfully, looking from one to the other.

Elise felt a major blush creeping up her neck.

Adam shook his head and never took his eyes from Elise. "I can't understand this compulsion to run away from me," he commented, sounding genuinely confused, "Is something wrong with me?"

Elise let out a little gasp. "Of course not," she blurted out.

"Oh. Well, that's good to know." Adam looked oddly pleased, but he didn't pursue the subject further. He turned to face Phil. "Ready for the rest of that football interview now?"

"I sure am."

"I'm going to leave you with your reporter, Phil," Elise said. She had to force the words past a giant lump in her throat. "Thanks for the flowers and — good luck on your recovery." She began to walk off toward the nurses' desk.

"I'll see you around school, Elise," Phil called out to her. She made a point of not turning around. She certainly didn't want to see Adam Tanner any more than she had to!

It was a tradition for Scott and Emily to jog together before dinnertime through Rose Hill Park. This afternoon they were dressed warmly and were feeling invigorated by the cold air.

"I can tell you have something on your mind, Em," Scott said as they passed the pond and went over the curved wooden bridge. "Do you want to let me in on it?"

Emily laughed. "I think you already know what I'm thinking about," she said. "Adam and Elise."

"And how to get them together," Scott finished for her. He was grinning and shaking his head in a knowing way. "Em, you are such a romantic optimist!"

Emily looked over at Scott and smiled. "I'm

glad I am. Our romance never would have gotten off the ground if I hadn't confronted you."

Emily was talking about the time she had waited for Scott in the school parking lot to straighten out all their misunderstandings. She had thought that he was interested in Heather Richardson, and he had thought she liked Jonathan Preston, and, well, it had been a mix-up that only required a lot of communication.

Emily was convinced that communication was the only thing missing in the fracas between Adam and Elise.

"You see, Adam thinks that Elise rejected him because she didn't like his looks or something," she told Scott. They were heading up a hill, and she was beginning to puff a little bit.

"And? That's not the reason?"

"Of course not. Elise had this terrific crush on Adam even before I ever fixed them up, but I didn't know a thing about it."

"That's hard to believe," Scott said, amused. "Something like that was going on, and *you* didn't know about it? Impossible."

Emily couldn't resist a small giggle. "I know, I really was slipping. If I'd been a true-blue Dear Abby I would have figured out who Elise had the crush on, but I still don't think it's too late for them."

"What do you mean? I thought Elise said that Adam has a girl friend now."

"I'm not so sure about that. Or even if he did decide he likes his next-door neighbor, maybe it was just an impulsive move, and he already regrets it. Otherwise why would he have kissed Elise the other night?"

"Em, be serious. Adam said that Elise was the most infuriating girl on this whole planet."

"Well, that, Scott, is my first clue," Emily said wisely. "Sometimes there's a very thin line between that sort of exasperation and love. It's just a hunch, but I think that's what we've got here. A boy who's crazy about Elise but is too confused to know what to do about it."

Scott didn't answer right away. They jogged along in silence for a while. Then he said, "You're incredible, Em. You're so good at solving other people's problems. But this time I'm not sure you can pull it off. I mean, you've been doing all you can, and still, they both say no to another date. . . ."

"We're going to arrange something," Emily said mysteriously. "You and I are going to put our heads together and get those two to admit they're interested."

Scott shook his head and let out a low whistle. "Well, I'm not convinced anything will work, but I'll help in whatever way I can."

"Good. That's exactly what I wanted to hear." Emily jogged on up the hill, a small, satisfied smile creeping over her face.

She would come up with a plan that neither Adam nor Elise could resist, and they'd be together before they knew what hit them.

Chapter
14

On Thursday morning before school, Fiona sat at the kitchen table, poking with little interest at a container of blueberry yogurt. Her attention was focused on a letter she'd received the day before from Lizzy, her best friend back in England.

She kept rereading the letter, trying to feel as thrilled as Lizzy had been when she heard that Fiona would be joining the National Ballet.

"It's the most wonderful news I've heard in a decade," Lizzy had written in her big, expressive handwriting.

> *"We'll be together again, just as we were all those years at Kingsmont. Only now we'll have the whole city of London to explore, and we won't be stuck in a little backwater seacoast town. . . ."*

Fiona smiled at that. She and Lizzy had often bemoaned the fact that Kingsmont was far away from any decent city. They'd often longed for the offerings of an urban area — theaters, shopping districts, good restaurants.

Well, now they would have it all. Work that they loved, their close friendship once again, and the marvelous city of London to live in.

"Being with the Ballet is such great prestige, Fiona, you cannot imagine. Everywhere we go, people respect us for our dancing. Patrons of the company throw grand parties, and all we need to do is attend and look the part of a ballerina. It's great fun."

Fiona felt her heartbeat quicken as she reread Lizzy's words. The ballet world she described sounded wonderful. How could Fiona ever have had any doubts about leaving Rose Hill?

". . . and naturally we are doing The Nutcracker *for the Christmas season,"* Lizzy's letter went on. *"I do wish you were here already, Fiona. . . ."*

Fiona sighed and folded the letter. She didn't have time to read anymore. It was almost time to leave for school.

She dipped her spoon back into her yogurt just as the telephone rang.

"Hi there, beautiful," Jonathan said when she

answered. "How would you like a chauffeur this morning? I've got Big Pink all revved up and ready to drive a lovely lady to Kennedy High."

Fiona frowned. "Why . . . that's awfully nice of you, Jonathan, but. . . ."

"You're not going to say no, are you?"

"As a matter of fact. . . ." She looked down at her feet, totally confused by her response. "I really wanted to walk this morning, Jonathan. It's important for my, you know, for me to keep in shape. For the National. . . ."

There was a long silence.

"Yes, of course, everything for the National," Jonathan said in a clipped way. "We certainly wouldn't want you getting out of shape."

"Jonathan, I'm sorry if you're upset."

"Are you, Fiona?" He sounded rather angry. "It seems to me you've been acting awfully cool lately. To me, especially."

"Oh, no," she protested. "I don't mean to be."

"Well, it's been happening that way." He made a funny sound, almost an impatient growl. "Oh, let's not get into this on the phone, all right? I'll see you later."

And he hung up without a good-bye.

Fiona drew in a deep breath and wondered what was happening. She didn't think she was treating Jonathan any differently than usual. She really would have to pay more attention to her behavior.

After all, they had less than two weeks left. And then she'd be far away, an English girl once more, a *corps* member of the National Ballet in London.

She was tempted to call Jonathan back and apologize. Maybe she'd even accept his offer of a ride to school.

But then she changed her mind. She stretched her neck to see out the window as she tossed away the uneaten portion of her yogurt. She would enjoy being outdoors. The weather looked cold but sunny, with just enough breeze to make her feel invigorated. The walk to school would do her good.

Adam Tanner sat alone in the sunny breakfast room of the big house on Warwick Terrace, picking at his scrambled eggs. He hadn't had much of an appetite in days. He got up and helped himself to a cup of coffee and sat back down in front of the tall window that looked out over the street.

He closed his eyes for a moment and tried to picture the maze of residential streets that wound through Rose Hill, wondering which one was Everett Street. He'd never been to Elise Hammond's house, but he knew she lived on Everett Street because he'd been foolish enough to look it up in the telephone directory.

He slapped his palm against his forehead. He'd done a lot of foolish things since he first met Elise Hammond, and he really couldn't understand why he got so agitated over a green-eyed girl who was always running away from him.

From the moment he met her he'd been intrigued. At first he just thought she was exceptionally pretty, with her dark curls and sparkling green eyes. But when she showed such interest in the

114

Animal Rights League, and then when she knocked over all those displays, he knew he was hooked. He'd been really sorry when she ran away before he could ask her for a date.

It had been the same when she had the mishap with Scott's locker. Even then Adam hadn't known her name, but he hadn't been able to get her out of his mind.

And then when he'd kissed her so impulsively in Miss Clement's garden, and she'd responded the way she did, he'd begun to think she cared for him. He'd been so sure . . . but he must have been wrong.

A light tap at the window brought Adam out of his reverie. Kelly stood there, jumping up and down, her auburn curls bouncing.

"G'morning, Adam," she chirped when he went to the door. "Can you give me a ride to school today? Mom left without me."

"And you're too lazy to walk?" Adam asked with a smile.

"I'm not lazy," she said. "It's just that I'd rather get a ride with my handsome next-door neighbor." With a toss of her head, she followed him inside and sat down beside him at the glass-topped breakfast table.

"Be serious," Adam growled. "It's too early in the morning for jokes, squirt."

"No joke. Haven't you ever noticed I have this major crush on you?" Kelly helped herself to a muffin from a nearby bread basket.

"You're too young to have a crush." Adam looked at her sternly.

"I am not. I'm fourteen. And you know I look older."

Adam moaned. It was definitely much too early for this. "Give me a break, Kelly."

"Okay," she said cheerfully. "How are you today?"

"Fine."

"You don't look fine to me. You've been moping around for a couple of weeks now. What happened to make you so sad, anyway?"

He let out a low chuckle. "What makes you think I'm sad about anything? Maybe it's you, squirt. I don't get to see you often enough."

"Very funny. I know I'd never have such an effect on you." Kelly looked at him and nodded her head seriously. "But it is a girl, I bet. And I think I know who the girl is."

Adam drained his coffee cup. "Let's skip this discussion today, okay?"

"I think you should have some orange juice," Kelly said suddenly, getting up and pouring a small glass for him. "Here. Drink up. You need some vitamin C."

It was easier to drink the juice than to argue with Kelly. Adam drank. He didn't even notice that she was fixing him a plate with more scrambled eggs until she had set it down in front of him.

"I don't want this," he protested.

"Eat up. You're still a growing boy. And you need brain food for all your great accomplishments in journalism."

Adam shook his head in surrender. He took a forkful of eggs.

"Listen, Adam, about that girl. . . ."

"What girl?"

"The one who's got you crazy," Kelly said lightly. "I know who she is. That Elise who was at Miss Clement's to help with the puppies. Am I right?"

"No."

Kelly was looking at him earnestly. "I wanted to tell you something important. I told a lie to Elise."

"What do you mean?"

"Adam, when we were riding in her car with the puppies, I didn't know she meant anything to you, honestly. I just felt like making up a story, so I told her that we — you and I — were going out. And that we might go to the Christmas dance together."

Adam stopped eating and stared at Kelly. "Why'd you do a stupid thing like that?"

She shrugged and looked ashamed. "I don't know. Wishful thinking, I guess. She was asking questions and it just sort of popped out. I'm sorry if I caused any trouble, Adam. I really didn't know about you and Elise then."

"There's nothing to know," he said gruffly.

"Boy, you're stubborn! But listen, what I wanted to say was, do you want me to tell Elise that I was lying? I don't want to be the cause of any trouble between you two. . . ."

"Don't worry about it. You weren't the cause of anything. There was trouble between us long before that, Kelly." Adam put down his fork and looked straight into Kelly's eyes. "Anyway, I'm sure she didn't believe a word you said."

"Oh." Kelly looked relieved.

"And I'm not going to talk about this anymore, squirt, so let's get going." Adam stood up and pushed away his plate. He was surprised to see that he had eaten a good portion, after all.

He reached out and ruffled Kelly's hair. "I'm glad you came over to cheer me up this morning. I was feeling kind of lonely."

"So you're sure?" Kelly persisted as Adam slipped into his coat. "You're sure you don't want me to explain things to Elise?"

"Forget about it," Adam said. "She's going to the Christmas dance with some football player named Phil, and she couldn't care less about me."

Chapter
15

On Thursday morning Elise and Emily were standing in the quad, stamping their feet and moving around to beat the cold, when Diana Einerson came flying toward them, her long blonde hair streaming out behind her.

"I'm glad I found you two," Diana called out.

"What's the matter, Di?" asked Emily.

"It just occurred to me," Diana said, "that we've been so busy planning the dance that we still haven't made final plans for a party for Fiona."

"Oh, you're right," Elise said. "Fiona's going-away party. We've got to have something really special."

"Yeah. What did you have in mind, Diana?" Emily said.

"Well, it's got to be this Saturday night because Holly and I are leaving for Montana right after the dance. Can you both make it?"

"Sure," Emily said. "Scott and I will be there. Elise, too, right?"

Elise made a comical face. "Of course. I haven't got any hot dates planned yet. As a matter of fact, my Saturday nights are free for the next year."

Diana looked worried. "Does that mean you won't be going to the dance, Elise?"

Elise shrugged. "No, I'm planning to go alone. But that's okay. Don't worry about me, Di. I'm fine." She pointed to the red and white button that she still wore on her jacket. "Independent, that's me," she joked.

Emily said nothing but was watching Elise's expression very carefully. Emily knew that Elise wasn't really fine. She also knew that her friend would love to go to the dance with a certain boy.

"Let's get back to Fiona's party," Elise said abruptly. "What plans have been made, Di?"

"Well, we want to try to surprise Fiona, of course," Diana said. "And Jonathan said he'll take care of getting her to my house. We've come up with a theme for the party so that we can get her all sorts of gifts to go along with it."

Diana took out a small notepad from her jacket pocket. "Let's see. I still need someone to make potato salad?"

"Fine. I can do that," Emily offered.

"And I can make a couple of desserts. How about brownies and chocolate chip cookies?" Elise asked.

"That would be great," Diana said, smiling. "And here's what we have planned for the party theme. . . ."

* * *

That afternoon Scott Phillips caught up with Adam Tanner in the boys' locker room right after a gym class basketball game.

"Hey, Tanner," Scott said casually. He sauntered over to Adam, who was sitting on the bench taking off his sneakers. "You know Jonathan Preston, don't you?"

"Of course," Adam said. "Who doesn't? Preston's a great guy."

"Yeah. Well, do you know his girl friend? Fiona Stone?"

Adam glanced up at Scott. "Sure. Jeremy Stone's sister. Why?"

"There's a bunch of us planning a good-bye party for Fiona this Saturday night. She's going back to England to study ballet professionally." Scott said. "Would you like to come?"

"Me? Why me?" Adam looked really curious. "Somebody needs a story written for the newspaper about departing ballerinas?"

Scott laughed. "No, not at all. We just thought you might enjoy it. The more the merrier, you know. It'll make Fiona feel really special if a big crowd shows up to wish her well."

"Uh, sure. Why not?" Adam said. "Where and when is this party?"

Scott gave Adam the details and went tearing out of the locker room to find Emily.

"Well, can he come?" she asked the minute Scott caught up with her.

"Yeah. He'll be there," Scott said.

"He's not bringing that girl friend of his, is he?"

"No," Scott said. "I know how to follow instructions, Emily. I told him it was only for Kennedy seniors, except for Fiona."

"I love you!" Emily declared, reaching up to plant a triumphant kiss on Scott's cheek.

At eight o'clock on Saturday night, Fiona was pouting as she and Jonathan drove along the streets of Rose Hill.

"Why won't you tell me where we're going tonight?" she kept asking. "If it's bowling or a movie, I'm overdressed."

She saw Jonathan steal a quick look at her as he drove. She had worn a pretty new dress with a dropped waist, even though she had no idea what their plans were.

"You're not overdressed," Jonathan said cryptically.

"That means it's not bowling or a movie." Fiona sulked some more. "Honestly. It's such a typically silly American thing to do, keeping secrets like this."

He continued to smile mysteriously until finally he pulled up in front of the Einersons' house.

"Okay," he said.

"Okay what?" she demanded. At just that moment, the front door opened and a crowd of kids streamed out onto the front lawn.

"What's — what's this?" whispered Fiona, completely startled. She realized that her heart was pounding wildly.

"SURPRISE, SURPRISE, Fiona!" the whole crowd called out at once. As they came closer,

Fiona saw that they all were vigorously waving small American flags.

"Oh, my," was all Fiona could manage to say at first. She looked at all her friends and shook her head in disbelief. "I never guessed — " she said at last, wiping tears from her eyes. "I never dreamed anyone would do this for me. You are all so great."

"Don't be silly," Diana said. "How could we let you leave Rose Hill without a special send-off?"

Jeremy stepped up to take the first of many photos. "You can weep if you want to," he said seriously. "That'll make great photojournalism. I'm putting together an album for you, Fi."

"Come on, get out of the car," Scott ordered. "We want you to come inside. It's time to PARTY."

They all trooped inside, and in the Einersons' large living room, they settled Fiona into a chair that had been decorated like a throne. Dee placed a fancy gold crown on Fiona's head.

"This crown represents your future home, England, where you have to be loyal to your Queen," she said. "And it represents the world of ballet where we know you'll be dancing many parts as a princess or a fairy with a sparkling tiara."

"Oh," Fiona said in a tearful voice. "I can't believe any of this. It's all so beautiful."

"Fiona," Dee went on, "before our party gets underway, we'd like to present you with some gifts to remember America by."

Fiona felt her eyes completely misting over.

Scott approached the throne and handed Fiona a Baltimore Orioles baseball cap. "What could be more American than baseball?"

"Oh, how perfectly lovely," Fiona said, taking the hat with trembling fingers.

"And here's something you don't have in England," said Elise. "The incomparable Mickey Mouse and his girl friend Minnie." Elise gave Fiona a huge T-shirt from Disney World emblazoned with the animated characters.

"I love it," Fiona said. "I shall wear it to ballet class."

"Put it on now," Jeremy said, snapping a picture. "We want a complete album from this party, Fi."

She pulled the T-shirt on over her dress. It came almost to her knees, and she pranced around in it, clowning. Then she replaced her crown with the baseball cap and reclaimed her throne.

"More gifts, more gifts," Emily called out.

Diana stepped forward with two rolled-up posters. "You'll need to decorate your new quarters when you get to London, so here are two all-American boys to take with you."

Diana unrolled one of the posters, and all the girls oohed with approval at the sight of a larger-than-life Tom Cruise.

"Thoroughly appropriate," Jeremy declared, taking another picture.

Fiona unrolled the other poster, and her laughter rang out through the Einerson house. This one was of Rambo, machine gun and biceps and all.

"We couldn't let you go back without the American hero," Diana said.

"Oh, how gloriously tacky," Fiona said, still choking with laughter. "I promise to put it up. Thank you, Diana. I'll feel right at home with these on my walls."

Other gifts came along in quick succession. Fiona received an Annapolis pennant from Matt Jacobs, a Statue of Liberty key ring from Ben, a replica of Plymouth Rock from Marc. There was a sketch of the Boston Tea Party, a postcard of Niagara Falls, and a small statuette of the Liberty Bell. She received a cowboy hat from her brother Jeremy, which she quickly popped on on top of her baseball cap.

Susan and Amy Atkinson presented Fiona with a large jar of chunky peanut butter. "We know you love the stuff," Amy said, "and although peanut butter is an American staple, we thought it might be hard to get in England."

"Thank you," Fiona said sadly. "Thank you all for these fabulous gifts. What a lot of thought went into them!"

And finally, there was an earthenware jar of Vermont maple syrup from Jonathan.

"We always planned to drive up to see Vermont," Jonathan said wistfully when he presented the syrup. "We'll never be able to do it, now."

"No," Fiona said in a sad whisper. "I'm sorry we never made it. . . ."

"*Stop*! No sadness allowed tonight," declared Matt Jacobs. "This is a night to party. Tomorrow you can cry."

Diana sat down on the arm of Fiona's throne and gave her a hug while Jeremy continued to snap pictures. "We're going to miss you so much," Diana said, wiping her eyes.

"Hey, no sniffling allowed!" declared Ben.

"Everyone will feel better after some food, I'm sure," declared Matt. "And I can vouch for the all-American dish Pamela made. Scrumptious apple brown Betty."

"Sounds fattening," Fiona said, smiling through her tears. "But it also sounds irresistible."

"You're not in England yet," Jonathan commented dryly. "Can't you eat without worrying about calories for once?"

Fiona turned her head sharply and gave Jonathan a long, cold stare. She was about to say something sharp and biting, but she bit on her lip instead. After all, she didn't want to ruin the party for everyone else. She forced herself to smile.

"You're absolutely right," she said in an exaggerated tone. "Tonight I'll not worry at all about calories."

And then, without waiting for Jonathan, she marched off toward the dining room where the food was set up.

Chapter
16

Fiona's party was turning out wonderfully, Elise thought. It had all the excitement and spirit of a holiday party, and yet it was true to its all-American theme.

The music was pure American rock. The food was all-American cuisine. But the decor, Elise noted with satisfaction, was typically Christmas. She went wandering through the pine-scented rooms by herself, feeling restless.

The Einersons had put their Christmas tree up early, so that its soft white lights lent a quiet, romantic glow to the big living room. An angel winked from the top of the tree, and beneath it were brightly wrapped Christmas gifts. The entire house was festive, from the mistletoe hanging in almost every doorway to the garlands of ever-green on the fireplace mantel.

In the dim, quiet entry hall, Elise reached out and touched the sharp, prickly leaves of some holly arranged in a vase. She fingered the tiny red berries morosely and wished she could feel more excited about the holiday season.

Just then the doorbell rang, and Elise opened the door without hesitation.

Adam Tanner stood on the doorstep, illuminated by the muted hues of the outdoor Christmas lights. He was all red and green and silver and blue, looking like a Christmas tree himself.

"Hello, Adam," Elise greeted him, smiling broadly. She couldn't help it, she was so glad to see him.

"This is getting to be a regular event, running into you," Adam said, grinning at her.

Still standing out on the doorstep, Adam took off his hat. He'd been wearing a Texas Stetson that made him look very rugged and outdoorsy. The minute he took it off, the cold wind whipped his hair all around. Elise could see that his cheeks were bright red from the cold.

"Can I come in?" he asked. "I was invited, you know."

"Oh, of course. I'm sorry. I don't know where my brain is!" Flustered, she opened the door wider and shivered as some of the frigid air came blowing in behind Adam.

Adam's sturdy frame seemed to fill the doorway and then the entry hall. Elise backed away from him almost by instinct. It didn't matter how attractive she found him. She was supposed to be getting over him, she reminded herself, but she couldn't tear her gaze away from his face. She felt frozen to the spot.

"You," Adam said calmly, slipping out of his

coat, "are standing under a sprig of mistletoe."

"Oh, no, I'm not!" Elise said quickly. But in spite of herself, she looked up and saw that it was true. She had backed herself, unwittingly, under the mistletoe.

"Don't even *think* about it," she said, remembering Kelly. But it was too late. With one quick stride, Adam moved forward and took Elise's face gently between his hands.

"Don't run away from me this time, Elise," he whispered just before he lowered his lips gently over her own.

Elise responded joyfully. She flung her arms up around his neck and hugged tight, quickly forgetting about Kelly. They fit together so perfectly, there couldn't be anything wrong with this kiss. Elise let out a soft moan and wished she could stay like this forever.

But she came to her senses at last and pulled gently away. It had been only a mistletoe kiss, nothing more. She knew that. After the party he'd go home to Warwick Terrace and his pretty girl friend next door, and Elise would be forgotten.

She couldn't be angry at Adam. She only felt sad that their kiss under the mistletoe would be the last one they'd ever have.

"Where are you going now, Elise?" Adam asked as she pulled away. "You promised you wouldn't run away." His eyes searched her face.

"I never promised! I have to. . . ." She tried quickly to think of something. "I promised Diana that I'd help in the kitchen. . . ."

Adam stared at her, looking surprised and hurt. "Okay, fine," he said in the echoing silence that followed her outburst. "I'll see you around, I guess."

"Yes," Elise said quickly. "I'm not going far, just to the kitchen — "

Before Elise could finish her sentence, Adam turned on his heel and went off toward the dining room to join the party. From where she stood, he looked like a very unhappy person.

Elise found Emily and Scott dancing to a slow song near the Christmas tree.

"Excuse me, you two," she said. "May I ask you something?"

"Sure," Emily said.

"Sure, Elise," Scott echoed.

Elise frowned. "Did either of you invite Adam Tanner to this party?"

Both Emily and Scott feigned surprise. "Adam is *here*?" Emily asked.

"Em, stop beating around the bush," Elise said. "Did you or Scott invite that boy?"

"Uh, well, it's possible that Scott might have mentioned the party to Adam."

"Yeah," Scott said. "Adam's a nice guy. I thought he'd be fun to have at a party like this."

"I'll just bet." Elise stared at her two friends, wondering if she should be upset with them or not. In the end, her good nature won out, and she managed to laugh a little bit at herself.

"You two are incorrigible matchmakers," Elise said. "I just don't know what I'm going to do with you."

"You're probably going to relax and enjoy the

party, Elise." Emily spoke like a true advice-giver. "That's what you ought to do."

"I will." Elise smiled bravely. "The only thing is, I'll have to be extra careful. I'll have to check out all the mistletoe and avoid it from now on."

This statement brought the wild result that Elise knew it would.

"What do you mean? What happened?" Emily was almost frantic with curiosity. "Are you kidding? Did you stand under some mistletoe? Did Adam kiss you — again?"

But Elise just smiled mysteriously. "I'm not talking," she said. "Not as long as you two keep playing sneaky tricks on me."

"Oh, Elise, I'm sorry," Emily said. "Tell me what happened."

"I want to go see how Diana's doing in the kitchen," Elise said, ignoring her friend's pleading look. "See you guys later."

In spite of her confusion, Elise felt an odd sort of calm somewhere down deep inside her. She couldn't help thinking that if a boy kissed a girl like that, maybe he did have some feelings for her, after all. Maybe she should just ask Adam outright why he kept trying to kiss her. That ought to settle it, one way or another. She made up her mind to try to talk to him before the night was over.

Chapter *17*

Fiona had finally settled down after the initial shock and was starting to enjoy her surprise party, when Ben stood up to make an announcement.

"Hey, everybody, listen up," he said, motioning for people to gather around him. "I almost forgot to tell you some incredible news I heard today."

"Well, what's the big excitement?" Mark asked.

Ben cleared his throat. "I bumped into this kid I know from Stevenson High," Ben said. "He told me that in the last few years, enrollment at Stevenson has been going way down."

"*That's* the news?" Jonathan spoke up.

"Shut up, Preston. No, the news is that they're going to close Stevenson down," Ben said. "It won't exist anymore after the new year."

"Really?" Jeremy whistled softly and scratched

his head. "That's quite surprising, closing a school down. Where will the students go?"

"Well, that's the interesting part," Ben answered with a grin. "Rumor has it that they're going to divide up the students. And roughly one third of them will be coming to Kennedy."

"Coming to Kennedy?" people repeated. "*Our* Kennedy??"

"But that's . . . that's unheard of," Dee exclaimed. "Piling a whole bunch of new students into Kennedy. How are we supposed to share our school with those guys?"

"Yeah. Those guys are our rivals," Marc said.

"That's right," Jonathan said. "They've been neck and neck with Kennedy in sports and academics. . . ."

"They have a great newspaper over there," Karen Davis, editor of Kennedy's school paper, put in. "I wonder what it will be like to have some of those people working on *The Red and the Gold*?"

"And at WKND, too," her boyfriend, Brian Pierson added. He was a disc jockey at the school radio station. "This sounds awful. They're going to step in and take over our school."

"I guess it doesn't matter whether we like it or not," Emily said. "If it really happens, we'll have to learn to grin and bear it."

The comments were growing more heated, when suddenly Fiona couldn't stand it anymore. She began to weep uncontrollably. She turned away from the group and buried her face in her hands, her narrow shoulders trembling.

"Fiona, what's wrong?" demanded Emily.

Diana put a finger to her lips and motioned for the group to move into another room. Diana, Dee, Holly, and Elise, as well as Jonathan, stayed behind.

"Tell us what's wrong," Elise said softly.

A few minutes went by while Fiona tried to control herself. When she finally spoke up, her voice was small and shaky.

"I wish I could be a clone," she said.

"Fiona, what on earth do you mean?" Holly asked gently.

Fiona spoke up a bit louder. "All this talk about Stevenson High and next year. . . . No matter how things work out with those kids, I won't be here to see what happens. And I can't stand it, I really can't stand the thought of not being here for all those exciting things."

"Oh, Fiona." Dee reached out and hugged her.

"So I wish I could be cloned," Fiona said, taking a tissue Diana held out. "Then I could go on and have my ballet career and still stay here in America, too."

As the girls sighed in understanding, Jonathan came and perched himself on the edge of Fiona's throne.

"You can't be cloned," he said. "I don't want to make you feel worse, Fiona, but you can't have your cake and eat it, too. It's a matter of making a choice, and you've already made yours."

Fiona looked up at Jonathan with tear-filled eyes. What was the matter with him? Why was he being so unsympathetic?

"You *are* trying to make me feel worse, Jonathan," she said in a dangerously low tone.

"I'm not," Jonathan assured her. "I just wanted you to face the facts and not spend your time in tears. Come on, Fi. This is *your* party. You're supposed to be enjoying yourself. Why don't you come and dance with me? I think I hear one of your favorite Talking Heads records playing — "

Jonathan reached out for her, but Fiona pulled away from him with an angry shake of her head.

"Don't touch me," she snapped. "I don't feel like dancing."

"Fiona, what's gotten into you?" Jonathan asked.

"Nothing," Fiona answered. "I just don't want your comfort or pity, Jonathan. You can't understand how I feel. You simply *refuse* to understand how I feel. . . ."

Jonathan's face blanched. He looked at Fiona with shocked, wounded eyes. And then he reached out and took her by the elbow.

"Let's talk about this in private," he said. He marched her away from the party and out to Diana's backyard. It was bitter cold and windy, but the cool air felt good on their flushed faces. They stood in the shelter of a big, leafless oak tree and faced each other squarely.

"Now," Jonathan said. "Let's get one thing straight. I don't understand how you feel? I happen to think I've been the most understanding person in the world these past few weeks."

"You would," Fiona snapped. "You think you can say a few meaningless, kind words and that passes for real understanding. Well, let me tell you — "

"No." Jonathan's voice thundered out. "Let me

tell *you*, Miss Fiona Stone, prima ballerina-to-be. I've had it with your snide remarks about Americans and about me in particular. This past week you've been extremely critical of me, Rose Hill, Kennedy High, and the United States in general."

"I haven't," Fiona said uncertainly.

"Yes, you have. And admit it, Fiona, you've been as cold as an ice maiden ever since you made your decision to leave for England. Always complaining about me, avoiding me whenever possible. It's been very obvious to me, anyway."

"That's not true," Fiona said, meaning it. "Why would I do a thing like that, when I love you so much . . . ?"

"I guess because you don't love me so much," Jonathan emphasized. "You didn't want to ice-skate with me, dance with me, ride with me, or even be alone with me while we were watching that movie the other night. How do you think all that makes me feel?"

Fiona moved to sit down on the edge of the patio. Jonathan came and sat down beside her, resting his head in his hands.

"It makes me feel like a terrible creep, a hanger-on whose presence is totally unwanted."

"Oh, Jonathan, no. . . ." She felt her heart twisting in a knot at the thought that she might have hurt Jonathan.

"Well, forget it," Jonathan said. "If I'm such a creep, then I ought to stay out of your life. I've always known that you put your ballet before me, anyway."

"And is that a crime?" Fiona asked uncertainly. "You know I'm a professional dancer. I never made any secret about that."

Jonathan stopped arguing and stared at her. "Well, maybe I'm tired of being a professional *loser*." He hesitated for a split second, and then said in a tired voice, "Let's just cancel the whole thing, Fiona."

"What . . . what do you mean?"

Jonathan's eyes left her face. He stared up at the dark December sky. "I mean, let's not go through this charade for the rest of your time here. It's not necessary for you to keep on pretending you're my girl friend when you don't want to be."

"But. . . ." Fiona felt genuinely confused. Her thoughts were whirling around so fast she felt dizzy.

"No buts, Fiona," Jonathan said. "We'll just cancel the rest of our plans for December. You won't have to go to the dance with me, or any other holiday parties. You won't even have to buy me a Christmas present!"

With that, Jonathan tipped his Indiana Jones hat graciously. Then he turned silently and walked off into the night without another word.

Fiona stood up and went to stand beside the big old magnolia tree, silent tears streaming down her cheeks. She shivered and hugged herself with her arms to keep warm. But her movement did nothing to stave off the bitter feeling of cold within, way down deep inside of her.

How had this happened? How and why had she alienated Jonathan Preston, the only boy she had ever loved? How had they gotten to this point where he had declared their romance was over?

She shivered again and walked around in a little circle, feeling alone and confused. A sliver of a moon hung suspended in the night sky, not enough for real light, but enough to make her feel even more sorrowful.

This was supposed to have been such a wonderful time, her last month here in Rose Hill. She and Jonathan were going to enjoy what little time they had left together and store up a lifetime of memories.

Instead, somehow she had destroyed it all. And she didn't have a clue as to how or why.

Chapter 18

"Poor Fiona," Emily said to Elise. "I still can't believe her going-away party ended like that."

The two friends sat in the bustling cafeteria of the Children's Hospital on Sunday, the afternoon after the party. Elise was on her half-hour break, and Emily had popped in to surprise her.

"It was a nightmare for Fiona," Elise said, squeezing a lemon into her steaming cup of tea.

"And no one knows exactly what happened," Emily said. "I mean, one minute she and Jonathan looked so in love, and the next — bam. He was gone."

"When Jeremy and Diana and I took Fiona home, she never stopped crying," Elise said. "Not even when we tried to get her to open up and talk a little bit. Oh, it's so sad."

Elise didn't say anything, but the abrupt ending to the party had been sad for her, too. She'd had those brave plans of confronting Adam Tanner while his kiss was still freshly imprinted on her lips, but she'd never had the chance. She hadn't even seen him again after that.

"Listen, Elise, I came by for a reason," Emily said casually. "I have something up my sleeve that I think you're going to like."

"What is it?" Elise asked. "Are you matchmaking again?"

"No, no," Emily assured her. "This is something to do with your passion for causes. There's someone who wants to meet you about a certain important charity project."

"*Oh*, really?" Elise perked up but looked at Emily suspiciously. "That's — interesting. What kind of project?"

Emily cleared her throat and continued. "I really don't know a whole lot about it, Elise. That's why you have to meet with her. All I know is, this person is pretty influential."

"I don't understand."

"You will. Just trust me, okay?"

Elise was amused but also intrigued. "You mean someone needs my help? Needs me to do some fund-raising or something like that?" she probed.

"Something like that," Emily said smoothly.

"Wow, I'm flattered." Elise reached out to put some butter on her roll. "You're sure you can't tell me the name of her organization, at least?"

"Sorry, but no. I just hope you're willing to meet with her, no questions asked. Are you?"

"Well, sure, I guess. I'd love a new project to work on."

"Then it's settled." Emily pushed her chair back.

"What is?"

"Can you meet with her tomorrow evening? For dinner?"

"Sure. But where?"

"At the Lakeside Inn. It's one of her favorite places."

"Oh." Elise was surprised. "Well, okay. I'll be there, but how will I know her?"

"Just ask the waiter to seat you at table fifteen, by the window."

"Emily, what's her name?"

But Emily had already turned down the hall. Elise stood there alone.

She sighed, closing her eyes to force out the image of her and Adam Tanner sharing a romantic evening at the Lakeside Inn.

"Hey, Tanner." Scott Phillips came around the corner of Adam Tanner's huge house and spotted Adam hitting practice balls against the wall.

"Hi, Scott," Adam said, grinning widely. "Great party last night. I had an especially good time utilizing the mistletoe."

"Did you?" Scott pretended to be unaware of Adam's misadventures with Elise. "Listen, I came to give you an idea for a story, Adam. Maybe a big one."

"You're kidding." Adam looked fascinated.

"No. There's a certain local VIP who wants to confer with you. . . ." Scott looked down at his sneakers and shuffled his feet as he tried to fabricate a realistic story.

"If you'll meet this guy at the Lakeside Inn tomorrow night, you'll get a great story on some big local news," Scott said in a rush. "I guess he'll expect you to buy him a dinner, but what the heck? It'll be well worth it, I assure you."

"You've got to at least tell me the guy's name," Adam said.

"I can't, Tanner. He's hesitant about talking to begin with. You've got to trust me on this one."

"Well, this is bizarre," Adam commented, swinging his tennis racket to serve another ball.

"Just be at the Lakeside Inn tomorrow night, eight o'clock, table fifteen."

Adam seemed to consider this for a minute. Then he shrugged. "You're right, what the heck. I have nothing to lose, do I? And if it's as good a story as you say, Pulitzer Prize, here I come."

"That's the attitude," Scott said, nodding his head with approval. He hoped this latest set-up of Emily's worked. He was getting tired of all this cloak-and-dagger intrigue. Emily the matchmaker would have to operate without him if this scheme failed.

Chapter
19

"Fiona, let me in! I need to talk to you!"

Fiona was lying facedown on her big four-poster bed, her head buried in pillows. She didn't feel like seeing or talking to anyone.

"Come on, Fiona. Please. You can't stay holed up in there forever. Let me in," Diana pleaded.

"Oh, all right," Fiona said, climbing off the bed. "But don't blame me if I'm awful company. I'd really rather be alone right now."

"This'll just take a second, I promise."

Fiona opened the door and frowned. "Why are you here, Di? I told you, I don't feel like talking."

"I know you don't, Fiona. But I'm worried about you, and I think it will be good for you to spend some time with a friend."

Fiona led Diana into her room, sat down tiredly on the plush carpeting, and pulled her knees up tightly to her chest. Diana plunked down on the floor beside her. Fiona looked around the room that she had grown to love so much over the past year. She had recently redone it. She had painted her walls a pale gold and hung outrageously bright drapes of green and gold in a sharp foliage pattern that matched the bedspread. She'd completed the look with dozens of baskets, all shapes and sizes, some hung on the walls, others resting on top of shelves.

"It's so depressing," Fiona said morosely. "I just redecorated my room, and now I have to leave."

"Fiona," Diana said seriously. "You're not thinking of changing your mind or anything, are you?"

Fiona considered that for a moment. "No. Absolutely not. I do wish I could have a clone, I really meant that, but if I have to choose, then, well, I have to choose my career at the National."

Diana sighed. "I was afraid you'd say that. Well, the big question now is, what's going on between you and Jonathan?"

Fiona stared down at the rug, running a finger through the thick woven strands. "I don't know. I honestly don't understand what's been happening."

Diana sat there silently, waiting for Fiona to say more.

"I guess . . . I have to admit that he's been great," Fiona said. "He's been supportive and loving and patient, all the right things. And somehow I kept wishing that he *wasn't* so nice and perfect all the time!"

"Aha. Why?" Diana asked.

"Well, because. . . ." Fiona became confused.

"Well, that's obvious, I think. It's because it will be so hard to leave him when I love him so much. . . ."

"So how did you get to this point, Fiona? Somehow, all that love went out the window, and you two had that horrible fight."

"I'm not sure." Fiona hugged her knees even tighter and tried to think. Her brain was fuzzy, just as her eyes were blurry from crying so long and so hard. She'd been trying to figure out what had happened all night long, and all she had decided was that somehow, she was to blame for the problems between her and Jonathan.

"Di," she said slowly, "Do you think I've been sort of cold to Jonathan these past weeks?"

Diana seemed to consider that. "From what I've seen, probably yes, a little bit. Remember how you wouldn't stay with him at the skating rink? That wasn't like you."

"I know. I wouldn't even kiss him that night! I kept finding fault with Jonathan. I was always looking for something to pick on — " Fiona broke off as other memories crowded in. "Why did I do all that? I was always saying things about 'you Americans. . . .' "

"Yes, I remember hearing you say that a few times," Diana said. "Putting Americans down, even when I knew you didn't feel that way. It was as though you were sort of removed from all of us already."

Fiona felt her heart take on a strange sort of rhythm, booming and pounding, like a machine, as she began to see the whole picture. She caught her breath and began to speak.

"Di, did you hear what you just said? I was sort of removed from everyone in Rose Hill. That must be exactly what I was doing! I was removing myself, distancing myself, just so it would be easier to leave when the time came!"

"Oh, Fiona, maybe you did." She put a comforting arm around Fiona's shoulders.

"I can't believe I did that," Fiona mumbled, feeling ashamed of herself. She had treated Jonathan badly, perfect Jonathan, who was always so kind to her. "Yes, it makes sense, now that I think of it. I really was cold to Jonathan, and it's a wonder he didn't break up with me long before this!"

"So that's what you fought about?" Diana asked. "Your coldness and your pulling away?"

"Yes," Fiona said, sniffling. Tears were beginning to make tracks down her cheeks. She turned her head, stretching her neck so that she could see Jonathan's eight-by-ten senior picture on her bureau. He looked so terrific in that photo; of course, he always looked terrific, to Fiona. What had she done? Was it too late to patch things up with him?

She jumped up from her spot on the floor. "I've got to go see him, Di."

"Well, he isn't at home. I know that. Jeremy and I just came from his house," Diana said.

Just in case, Fiona quickly dialed Jonathan's number. When his mother answered and said that he hadn't been home all day, her heart sank. She hung up the phone with a sigh and tried to think of where he might be.

"I think I know!" she burst out, turning to face

Diana. "I think I can find him! Listen, Diana, will you forgive me if I dash off on my bike now?"

"Of course. As long as you know what you're doing."

"I do now," Fiona said, clasping her friend's hand. "Thanks for talking to me, Di. I feel so much better now that you've helped me figure things out."

"Any time," Diana said, her face bright. "Good luck, Fiona."

The sky was turning to dusk just as Fiona arrived at Rose Hill Park. She rode her bike close to the big lake and parked it under a line of weeping willow trees. She was relieved to see Big Pink parked nearby.

The evening was cold, but Fiona had bundled up in her heaviest ski jacket, gloves, and a scarf. The outer part of her was warm enough; it was only on the inside that she still felt bleak and cold.

She walked across the frozen path toward the north side of the lake, then crossed the curved bridge and headed straight for the gazebo, the old wooden structure that had been in the park almost as long as the trees had.

He was there. Fiona's heart ached when she saw him — stooped over like an old man, pacing back and forth in the gazebo like a lion in a cage.

"Hello?" Fiona called out tentatively in a timid voice.

Jonathan whirled to face her. "What are you doing here?"

"Oh, Jonathan, I'm sorry. I've come to apologize," she began, but before she could get any

147

further, she began to cry.

"Apologize? What for, Fiona? Forget it. It's over."

"No!"

Fiona exploded and stamped her foot against the wooden steps. "I came all this way to say something, and I want you to listen."

Jonathan let out an impatient sound, but he didn't try to stop her from talking.

"Diana and I have just been talking, and I realize now what a terrible thing I've done," she said slowly and carefully. It was hard to get the words out because her voice kept breaking, but she kept on.

"I know I was awful to you and I don't blame you for breaking up with me. But, the truth is, I understand now why I was behaving like that, Jonathan. I needed to distance myself from you, simply because I love you so much."

"What? Fiona, what are you talking about?"

"Just what I said," she answered, trying to explain. "In a way I've been preparing myself to leave you. If I made things unpleasant between us now, it wouldn't be so hard when it came time to leave."

He stared at her. There was a long silence.

"I guess that makes sense. So you think that's why you kept finding fault with me?"

She hung her head, and a thick shock of hair fell onto her forehead. "It must be. Because I know I really love you."

"And that's why you started avoiding me? Are you sure you don't hate me?"

"Of course I'm sure."

Jonathan stood there looking at her, his face all scrunched up in the pale light that came from the lampposts.

"I don't know, Fiona," he began. "I have to think about this." He left the gazebo and went over to the edge of the lake where he stopped and stared into the dark, rippling water.

Fiona's heart twisted with sorrow. She had made her apology, but it hadn't done any good. Jonathan had still pulled away from her. He wouldn't forgive her.

She followed him down to the water's edge, but this time she was careful to keep her distance.

"I realize my explanation wasn't enough," she said in a small voice. "But I wanted to tell you, anyway. I guess I had hoped we could remain friends for the rest of my time here, but. . . ."

She broke down and could say no more.

After a moment's silence that seemed to go on forever, Jonathan turned to her.

"Look, Fiona, I've been here in the park most of the afternoon, feeding some stupid birds that forgot to leave for the winter. And I've been thinking."

He yanked his hat off and looked straight at her.

"I've been thinking about *Swan Lake*. . . ."

"*Swan Lake*?"

"Yeah. I looked it up in the library last week. And I thought, maybe Fiona will dance that ballet some day. Maybe even be the Swan Queen. . . ."

"I can't believe you looked it up in the library," she whispered.

"The point is, Fiona, that you're leaving me.

You're going to be — well, almost tearing off one of my limbs when you go away. And I keep trying to understand *why*. . . ."

"And you do, now?" she asked softly.

"Yeah, I guess I do, a little bit more. It's crazy but when I learned more about *Swan Lake*, I started to be so proud of you all over again. . . ."

"Oh, Jonathan," she whispered. She didn't move, but she was achingly aware of the distance between them. "I can't tell you how sorry I am for the way I've been behaving lately. I didn't intend for it to be that way. All I did was destroy our last days together."

Suddenly Jonathan started to move toward her. She took a tentative step forward herself. Then both of them threw any hesitation away. She flew toward Jonathan just as he strode over to be closer to her. He took her in his arms, holding so tight that she thought she would break. She began to cry with happiness, but he reached down and, with a forefinger, gently wiped the tears away from her cheeks.

"No more tears, Fiona," he said in a husky voice. "We both love each other, and we have just this short time left. So why do we waste it like this? Fighting, having misunderstandings, crying. . . ."

"Yes," she said breathlessly. "I agree. I agree."

"Let's make a vow," Jonathan said, hugging her fiercely. "We *will* enjoy the time we have left. You don't have to leave until New Year's Eve, so we can at least enjoy the Christmas formal dance, and all the rest of it. . . ."

"Yes, oh, yes." She tipped her face back to receive his kiss. They clung to each other, kissing as if tomorrow did not exist. Fiona cried no more tears. They had vowed that there should be no sorrow.

A cold wind whipped at their faces, but together they seemed to make a tight circle that shut out the bitter air. Fiona could hear a gentle lapping sound from the lake, and the sighing of evergreen trees as winter winds blew through the branches.

When they finally pulled apart, they walked along the lake's edge with their arms tightly intertwined. It felt wonderful to be close to Jonathan again. And Fiona knew she'd never do anything again to endanger their love.

She was singing her swan song here in Rose Hill, she thought. She wanted to do it right. She was a performer, after all, and it was a ballet tradition, after the final curtain calls and bows, always to leave the stage smiling.

And so Fiona smiled.

Chapter
20

Elise's hair was soft and shining, and her makeup looked just right, she thought. She examined herself in the bedroom mirror one last time before leaving. Tonight was the meeting that Emily had arranged for her. By now, Elise's curiosity had mounted to anxious anticipation. She couldn't wait to see who she'd be meeting.

She ran some blush across her upper cheekbones and declared herself ready. In her cream-colored sweater and black wool pants she thought she looked casual, but professional, too. She put tiny gold hoops through her ears for the final touch and went downstairs and out the door.

She took her time and drove slowly to the Lakeside Inn, enjoying the scenery as she went. This was almost as good as going to the Christmas formal with some fantastic boy, wasn't it?

Well, not quite. Even Elise couldn't fool herself that much. She let a little sigh escape from her lips as she drove along the dark hemlock-lined road to the Inn. She still had romantic visions of what it would have been like to go to the dance with Adam Tanner, but she forced herself to squash those thoughts. For the rest of the way she concentrated on the meeting that was ahead of her insead of about what might have been.

She felt very sophisticated as she handed the keys to the car to the boy in the red vest. Hmmm, she thought, valet parking. Kennedy's Christmas Dance is really going to be posh.

Her shoes clicked across the front terrace of the Inn as she approached the door. A receptionist smiled at her from the front desk. "Can I help you?"

"Yes. I'm meeting someone at table fifteen," Elise said. The receptionist motioned for a waiter to escort Elise to her table.

Someone was playing a piano near the bar, and the soft notes mingled with the sounds of tinkling glassware and the low buzz of quiet conversation. The restaurant smelled pleasantly of perfume, fresh flowers, and delicious food. Elise smiled as she followed the waiter across the busy dining room of the restaurant.

But her smile froze when they neared the table. At first she thought she was seeing things.

Adam Tanner was sitting there at table fifteen. Elise gasped as she began to see the light.

There was no one who needed Elise for a charity project. There was no one but Adam Tanner! Emily's story must have been one big fake just to lure Elise here . . . but for what?

For another disastrous date with Adam?

"I don't believe this," Elise said out loud. She was hiding behind a pillar where Adam couldn't see her. She had to decide, right then and there, what to do.

She could walk out, and Adam would never be the wiser. He'd never know she'd been there at all. She didn't have to face him, not after all that had happened between them.

And there had been so much! All those klutzy episodes. The idea that Kelly was his girl friend. The fact that he had kissed Elise twice even though he had a girl friend.

Her face was burning hot. Elise stared at Adam from her hiding spot. He looked terrific, as usual. But what should she do? Could she face him now and enjoy herself with him?

It was Elise's intelligence and good sense that decided it, in the end. She realized that she liked Adam — liked him a lot, as a person, and not just a "crush" — and wanted him as her friend, if that was possible. Besides, there were a lot of unanswered questions racing through her mind. And so she admitted to herself that she didn't *want* to leave.

"Is this seat taken?" she asked shyly when she was right beside Adam's table.

"Huh?" He looked up at her in amazement, and it seemed to Elise that his confidence and poise disappeared instantly. His face looked boyish and shy.

"I know just what you're thinking," Elise said nervously. "What's *she* doing here?"

"Kind of," he admitted. He was shaking his head in disbelief.

"It looks to me as though Emily Stevens pulled a cute little trick on us," Elise said. "I'm supposed to be meeting some mystery guest here at table fifteen."

Adam merely stared for a moment. Then, as Elise sat down across from him, he managed a smile. The smile grew wider and wider, and suddenly he dissolved into laughter.

"Emily must have had Scott in on this trick," he said between laughs. "Scott told me there was a Pulitzer Prize story waiting here for me if I took some man to dinner. . . ."

Elise was laughing hard, too. It was so implausible that they both should fall for Emily's scheme. And yet they had, and here they sat alone with each other at table fifteen in the Lakeside Inn.

"Look you certainly don't have to have dinner with me," Elise said quickly, leaning forward in her seat. "I'll understand if you'd rather not."

Adam sobered up and sat back in his chair, staring at Elise with soul-searching brown eyes. "On the contrary," he said. "I'd love to have dinner with you. You're the one who's always running away from me. Perhaps you'd like to leave."

"Certainly not," Elise managed to say. "I'd love to have dinner with you. As a matter of fact, I tried to find you at the party the other night, but I never had a chance."

Adam's eyes lit up with amusement. "I was waiting for you under the mistletoe, Elise," he teased.

She stared at him. "That's it! That's what I

don't understand about you," she said. "You seem to be so sincere, so honest. . . ."

"I am."

"But you go sneaking around stealing kisses whenever your girl friend isn't around!" She pointed a finger at him. "What kind of person would do that?"

"My *girl friend*?" The look of amusement quickly disappeared from Adam's face. He leaned forward and frowned. "You don't mean. . . . Are you talking about Kelly?"

"Yes."

For a moment he looked too surprised to speak. Then he said, "You mean that's what this has been all about? You were running away from me all the time because you thought I was being unfaithful to Kelly?"

"Yes," Elise said. "Well, almost all the time. In the beginning, at the Garden Room, it was for another reason. But once I met Kelly, and she told me all about going out with you. . . ."

"You believed her!" He slapped his forehead. "I never thought anybody would believe anything Kelly says. Elise, she's just a kid with a big imagination. She's been making up stories since I first met her."

"She's not your girl friend?" Elise asked uncertainly.

"No, no way,' he said. "She's like a little sister to me. She made up that whole story, Elise. I don't know exactly what she told you, but I'm sure none of it was true."

Elise was stunned. She'd never thought that

Kelly might be lying, because the story had sounded plausible.

"She even told me you were taking her to the Christmas dance."

"That kid! I'm telling you, she'll make up anything." He shook his head. "So that's what made you run away. If only you'd told me before now. I thought you hated me."

"Oh, no. Just the opposite." She began to blush furiously. Just then the waiter came over to bring them menus.

Adam studied his, avoiding her gaze. "So, what do we do now? I think I'd like a pasta dish. How about you?"

"Uh — well, sure, I'm hungry, but. . . ."

"So let's do it." He grinned mischievously. "That is, if you think we can get through a meal without you spilling water on me. Or coffee. Or a lighted candle. . . ."

"I think I can manage that," Elise said, laughing. "Ordinarily, I'm not clumsy at all. That was only because you — " She stopped, horrified at what she'd almost said.

"Yes?" Adam prompted. "Only because I what?"

Elise didn't answer. She was looking down at the tablecloth and trying to think of a way out of this one.

Suddenly Adam's hand came across the table and captured hers.

"Come on, Elise. Can't we finally start to be honest with each other?"

"Oh, I don't know."

"Elise, tell me. Why did you suddenly become klutzy?"

"Well, to be truthful, I sort of thought you were . . . well, um, interesting-looking, that day in the mall. You know, cute. And you were so involved in the Animal Rights League thing and. . . ."

"You mean . . . you mean you had a *crush* on me, Elise?" He kept his face straight, but she could see the merriment behind his eyes. He was really enjoying this.

"No, no, nothing so dramatic as that — " She finally met his gaze head on. It was more than she could stand. She was sure his dark brown eyes could see right through her to the truth.

"Okay, yes. Yes!" she admitted. "I did have a crush on you. Silly of me, wasn't it?"

"No," he said in a low voice. "Not silly at all."

Adam leaned forward intently. "I have to confess something, too." he said. "Right from the start, I thought you were pretty adorable. Really. Especially when you knocked all the dog bones over, I was thinking, that's my kind of girl."

"You were?"

"Yes. Even after you emptied out Scott's locker."

"Oh, please, don't bring that up!"

He was silent for a moment. Finally he let go of her hand.

"Here's what I think," Adam said amiably. "We have a lot to learn about each other, and I have a feeling we both want to try. Emily must have arranged this because she wanted us to give each other a brand-new chance. So why don't we just do that — with no past memories. Just a whole new start."

"I'd love that," Elise said. She felt so happy that she thought she might explode. This was what she'd been hoping for ever since she first met Adam — a chance to get to know him better. It was hard to believe that so many misunderstandings had kept them apart.

"So, now that we have all the major problems straightened out, can we order dinner?"

"As long as we're here to learn things about each other, I have something to tell you," Elise began after the salad had been served. They had been laughing about a movie they'd both seen on TV a few nights ago, and she was feeling relaxed. The piano music in the background was soothing, and so was the view of the starry night sky out the picture window.

"What? You have a wild secret to reveal about yourself?" Adam pretended to look shocked. "Something scandalous?"

"No." She laughed. "Sorry to disappoint you. I just wanted to tell you I went to the school library just to look up all the old school newspapers that had your articles."

"You did?" He looked pleased.

"You're a good writer," she said. "But more than that, I liked your subject matter. You wrote all about important, interesting issues, ones I'd like to be involved in, too."

"Hey, we do have a lot in common, don't we?" Adam said, looking directly into her eyes. "A future social worker, and a future writer specializing in social issues." Adam deftly speared a piece of cucumber with his fork. "Sounds like a pretty terrific combination to me."

Elise felt a rush of warmth washing over her. She raised her glass of Coke and proposed a toast.

"Here's to us, then," she said.

"Absolutely. To us."

His eyes never left her face as he drank. They sparkled with pleasure, and Elise knew her own eyes reflected the same emotions. She hadn't been so happy in a long time.

The evening was so perfect she could hardly believe it was real. It passed in a pleasant blur, softened by candlelight and the warm glow from the fireplace.

Finally, though, it was time to go.

"But we're in separate cars," he said sadly. "I wanted to take you home."

They compromised. Adam drove along behind Elise to her house. When they reached Everett Street, he got out of his car and went to sit in hers.

"This has been a terrific evening, Elise," Adam said in a low voice. His arm was draped over the back of the front seat, his hand close to her shoulders. "I'm so glad we finally cleared up those misunderstandings."

"Me, too," she said.

"And I'm glad Emily played her little trick." Tentatively Adam moved a little closer to her.

"I am, too." She moved a fraction of an inch closer to Adam. She breathed in and could smell his fresh, clean scent.

"Elise — " he began, but never finished whatever he planned to say. He lowered his mouth to hers. His lips felt cool and firm. She wound her arms around his neck and combed her fingers through his dark wavy hair.

Elise closed her eyes, spinning like a leaf in a whirlwind. She had the sensation that the world was twirling crazily.

And then she thought, this kiss felt even more right than the others; for the first time since they'd met, the circumstances were right and the feelings were genuine.

Adam pulled back just a tiny fraction in order to look at her. "I've been dreaming of this ever since I first saw you," he said. "I only wish you hadn't run away all those other times."

"Shhh." She held a finger to his lips. "We promised, remember? No more raking up the past."

"That's right. The past doesn't exist." Adam kissed her forehead, the tip of her ear, the curve of her cheek. He continued to drop small kisses on her face until their mouths met again.

"Elise, is it too late to ask you to the Christmas formal?" Adam asked when they parted. "I know Phil Carey asked you, but I heard that his folks whisked him off to Florida, so — "

"Oh, Adam, he never really asked me. Is that what you thought?"

"Yes." He reached out and wound a lock of her hair around his forefinger. "Another misunder — " He stopped himself. "Right. No past. Now I'm asking you. So what do you say?"

Elise's heart was beating so loudly she was sure he could hear it. "Oh, Adam, I'd *love* to go to the dance with you," was all she could say.

Chapter
21

"Well, they're predicting snow for tonight," Emily announced, coming into Elise's bedroom. "I heard it on the radio on my way over here."

"Great," Elise said, her face practically buried in the mirror on her bureau.

It was the night of the Christmas formal, and the two girls were getting ready together at Elise's house.

"Hey, don't put on too much eyeshadow," Emily said, watching as Elise added colorful touches to her eyes. "A misty gray would be better. You don't want to look like a clown."

"I ought to make you look like a clown," Elise said playfully. "Paint your face purple for pulling that trick on Adam and me! Luring us both to the Lakeside Inn on such a pretext. You can't be trusted anymore, Emily Stevens."

"Hah." Emily plunked down on Elise's raspberry-colored bedspread. "Our plot worked, didn't it? Scott and I knew all along that you two just needed to be pushed together in the right setting."

"Yes, it worked," Elise conceded. Suddenly she gave her friend a big hug of gratitude. "Everything feels so good about this new relationship, Em. Adam and I have so much in common, it's positively spooky."

"You sure have," Emily said. "You're both stubborn."

"Very funny, Em." Elise glanced in the mirror and saw that her green eyes sparkled like winter stars. "I know it's early to say this, but I have this feeling that Adam and I were made for each other."

"I told you so!"

"I can't stand people who say I told you so," Elise countered. "Well, are we ready to put on our dresses?"

Emily was wearing a strapless dress of pale peach taffeta and Elise a rich green velvet. She wore small diamond posts, borrowed from her mother, and flashes of light sparkled from beneath her dark curls.

"That dress is gorgeous," Emily said, studying Elise.

"Thanks," Elise said. "And you look fantastic, like an angel."

She did, too. Elise thought of Emily as the angel who had managed to arrange things between her and Adam, making her date with him tonight possible.

When the doorbell rang, Elise sprayed on a tiny bit of perfume and ran downstairs, Emily close on her heels.

Elise's heart caught in her throat when she saw Adam coming toward her. He looked incredibly handsome in his black tux, and his brown eyes were approving as he turned toward Elise.

He seemed to catch his breath in pleasure at the sight of her. He said in a very low voice, "You look beautiful, Elise."

"Thank you," she said. She felt shy all of a sudden.

Adam held out a shiny corsage box with a big grin. She opened it with slightly trembling fingers.

"White carnations," Elise said with a smile. "Thank you. They're lovely."

"But don't you remember?" Adam said. He put a gentle hand on Elise's shoulder. "You were supposed to wear a white carnation to meet me once and you didn't, so this corsage is to make up for it."

"Oooooh," Elise said, laughing. "No fair! I thought we were starting out with a clean slate, Adam."

"We are," he said sheepishly. "All except for the carnations. I'm sorry, but I couldn't resist."

They laughed as they headed out the door, but grew quiet as they stepped outside onto a snow-covered Everett Street. The street lamps were surrounded by halos of light that illuminated the delicate snowflakes.

"How beautiful," Elise said, putting out her hand to catch a few swirling flakes. "Just exactly what we needed to make our dance perfect."

"It will be wintry, all right," Emily said, hurrying to get into Scott's Jeep before her carefully arranged curls came tumbling down.

On the ride out to the country, Elise and Adam snuggled together in the backseat to keep warm. Snow continued to fall, swooshing quietly against the windshield as they drove along.

The Lakeside Inn was everything that Elise had known it would be. On this night so close to Christmas, it had a radiance all its own. The old stone building was ablaze with light, and way down the long sloped lawn the surface of Lake Hemlock gleamed dark and velvety, serving as a mirror for the stars.

They pulled into the line for valet parking and jumped out, just as Big Pink drove up behind them.

"Wow, this place is gorgeous," Jonathan said as Fiona huddled close to him for warmth. Elise nudged Emily in satisfaction.

"Didn't we say that even practical old Jonathan would like it here?" Emily crowed.

"On a perfect night like this, practical old Jonathan would like it anywhere," Jonathan told them. But then he relented. "Okay, you're right, ladies. This is a pretty nice place. You guys definitely picked a winner this time around."

Adam took Elise's hand gently in his and led her carefully across the front terrace to the entrance of the Inn.

"I think *I* picked a winner this time around, too," Adam said in a low tone so that only Elise could hear. His words made her feel warm all over.

After they'd gone inside, Elise realized that many more people had shown up than anyone had dreamed would come. The ballroom was filled to capacity and then some, but luckily it was no problem to accommodate the extra arrivals.

"We're going to make a bundle," Jonathan told Elise. "That building fund will really have a great donation from us."

A wide smile spread over Elise's face. "Great," she said. She was glad her charity project had come to a good end, but she wasn't surprised to realize that she wasn't too interested in charity right now. She was walking hand in hand with Adam into a very special dance, and just then life held a great many other things besides her passion for good causes.

Their crowd of friends had taken one of the long tables near the stage where the D.J. was set up. Elise and Adam were greeted by Karen and Brian, Eric and Katie, Dee and Marc, Pamela and Matt, Ben and his date, and a host of other familiar faces.

The ballroom looked spectacular. The room was dim and low-ceilinged, creating an intimate atmosphere for the people who were sheltered inside, away from the snowstorm. A huge Christmas tree had been adorned with a muted set of lights, so that blues and silvers and golds gave off a holiday glow.

The dance began officially with a welcome from the guest disc jockey from WRRK. "The senior class of Kennedy High welcomes all of you!" he announced energetically. "What a night for you

Cardinals! The weatherman said snow, and sure enough we've got snow — enough to kick off a very special holiday season here! I have a request for this first record," the dj said. "A certain Jonathan wants to hear this one — " With a flourish he started up the music. The song was "Ballerina Girl."

As Elise watched Jonathan take Fiona's hand and lead her onto the dance floor, she thought her heart would break. She stood in silence with everyone else watching the graceful Fiona spin around in Jonathan's arms.

Jonathan himself broke the spell. "No sadness allowed tonight," he called out. "Come on, you guys, get out here and *dance*."

At that, many of the couples stood up and moved to the dance floor.

"So," Adam said, looking into Elise's eyes. "Can you dance or what?"

"Can I dance?" she scoffed. "Just try me."

They clasped hands and went out to the brightly polished dance floor. There, under softly glowing lights and in the spell of the Lakeside Inn, Elise realized her dream of slow dancing with Adam Tanner.

When the music had ended and another song began, Adam gave her hand a little tug. He urged her toward the big glass doors that led out to the terrace.

"I have something on my mind," he said simply, and she followed him with curiosity. They stepped out on the terrace and immediately felt the bracing cold of the winter night. They were protected from the snowstorm by a small awning, but the wildly whirling flakes were all around them anyway, whitening the dark country sky.

"Brrr. What's on your mind?" Elise asked, shivering and rubbing her arms. "It had better be good."

"It's this," Adam whispered, folding Elise into his arms so that she no longer felt the cold wind on her bare arms.

She brought up a hand to his neck, and she felt the quickening of his breath as their lips met. Their kiss was a dizzying contact that seemed to signify that they had found each other at last.

They were pressed together so tightly Elise could hardly tell where her heartbeat left off and Adam's began. She could hear the music drifting out from the ballroom, but it seemed miles away.

And off in the distance, Lake Hemlock lay silent and dark, just as it had the day Elise first set eyes on it, the same day she had been standing here on this terrace, dreaming.

So dreams can and do come true, Elise thought.

"Okay," Adam said happily, releasing his hold on her. "All is well. I wanted to see if you were going to run away from me this time, Elise."

She smiled and gently touched his cheek with her hand.

"Never, Adam," she whispered. "Never again."

Coming Soon. . .
Couples Special Edition
SEALED WITH A KISS!

"Hey," Katie said, checking her watch. "We still have a few minutes before the bell. Why don't we hang out at our old spot on the quad and see who else comes by?"

"That's a great idea, Katie," Eric agreed.

The quad was a very busy place, especially in the spring and fall, and Katie and her friends were regulars there. At the start of the school year they'd taken over the "territory" originally staked by Ted, Phoebe, Chris, Woody, and Peter, who were in last year's top senior crowd.

As the four rounded the corner, identical frowns crossed each of their faces. Some girls, none of whom Katie recognized, and a few boys in Stevenson jackets had taken over their space.

"Hey, that's our cherry tree!" Katie exclaimed, tossing her red ponytail indignantly.

"And those are our benches!" Eric growled.

They looked at each other, then turned sheepishly toward Greg and Molly. They all burst out laughing. "Listen to us!" Katie exclaimed ruefully. "You'd think we owned this place."

Katie and Molly giggled, and Eric threw his hands up in defeat. Just then the warning bell rang. "We'd better hurry," Molly said to Eric.

Katie knew she should go back to her own homeroom, but instead she lingered at the edge of the quad. One of the Stevenson girls was still sitting on what, until this morning, had been the gang's bench, and Katie couldn't help staring. The girl was flashy and beautiful. But what froze Katie in her tracks more than the girl's clothes and makeup was her expression. She was looking around the quad like she was planning to completely take it over. Was this girl an exception, or were all the Stevenson kids like her? Katie couldn't help wondering if the school merger between Kennedy and Stevenson would really be so easy after all.

It's a Night to Remember...

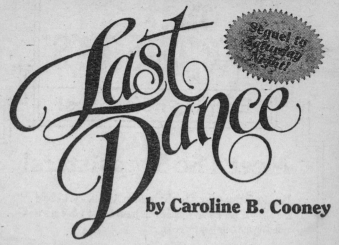

Last Dance

by Caroline B. Cooney

Sequel to Saturday Night!

Happiness and heartbreak are in the air. Eight months have passed since that special, memorable Autumn Leaves Dance. Now it's June, time for the last dance of the school year. Anne, wiser and more beautiful than ever, just wants to survive it. Beth Rose is more in love than ever...but wants Gary to fall in love with her, too. Emily, her safe world suddenly shattered, turns to Matt to make it right. Molly has been rejected, and she's out for revenge. Kip has been having the time of her life, and hopes the dance will be the perfect ending to the school year.

It will be romantic for some, heartbreaking for others...but above all, a dance the girls will never forget!

Look for it wherever you buy books!

$2.50 U.S./$3.95 CAN